MARIE-HÉLÈNE LEBEAULT
AUTHOR OF THE EVERS SERIES

THE QUEST

— FOR THE —

EMERALD
RATTLEBACK

DEFENDERS OF THE REALM - BOOK ONE

First published by Beaches and Trails Publishing 2023
Copyright © 2023 by Marie-Hélène Lebeault

First edition
Ebook: 978-1-990656-93-4
Paperback: 978-1-990656-92-7
Hardcover: 978-1-998386-27-7

Editing by Rachael Lammie
Proofreading by Alli Wait
Cover by Miblart

BEACHES AND TRAILS
PUBLISHING

ABOUT THE AUTHOR

Marie-Helene Lebeault lives in Quebec, Canada and is the mother of two young adults. A retired teacher, she now spends her days writing, translating academic manuals, and lending her voice to corporate training videos. She enjoys reading, hiking, and going to the beach. She is also an avid rollercoaster fiend and is on a mission to visit all the Six Flags amusement parks with her daughter. Every year, she travels for three weeks on a solo adventure to a new part of the world.

Follow on Social Media, she'd love to hear from you!

Website Email Newsletter

facebook.com/mhlebeaultauthor

x.com/mhlebeault

instagram.com/mhlebeault

amazon.com/author/mhlebeault

bookbub.com/authors/marie-helene-lebeault

goodreads.com/mhlebeault

linkedin.com/in/mhlebeault

tiktok.com/@mhlebeaultauthor

youtube.com/@mhlebeault

ALSO BY THE AUTHOR

The Chronicles of the Starborne Cadets

Stars Beyond Realms

Shadows of Orion

Echoes of the Void

The Nebula's Heart

The Starborne Paradox

Defenders of the Realm

A Journey to Power

The Quest for the Emerald Rattleback

A Summer of Discovery

The Quest for the Sacred Tree

A Summer of Opposites

The Quest for the Phantom Feather

A Summer of Courage

The Quest for the Kraken's Ink

A Summer of Destiny

The Quest for the Cursed Mirrors

The Evers Series

The Ancestors' Key

The Academy

The Time Walker

The World Jumper

Blood Magick Trilogy

The Blood Mage

Blood Magick

Blood Legacy

Standalones

Clarity Castle

What Happens Next?

Ghost Stories

Holiday Shifters

Echoes of Tomorrow

Utopia

Picture Books

Fairy Grandmother: Millie Goes to Antarctica

Fairy Grandmother: Millie Goes to the North Pole

Fairy Grandmother: Millie Goes to China

Fairy Grandmother: Millie Goes to Africa

(Also available in French, Spanish, German, and Italian)

CHAPTER
ONE

Summer clung to the bright skies and green fields, but Herja felt a chill in the morning that showed autumn was sneaking up on them. She rubbed her arms as she watched the dawn peek over the mountains to the east of the Institute.

"Herja," a voice called behind her. "What are you doing out here so early?"

Headmasters Twila and Valiant strode up beside her, arm-in-arm as usual. Both were grey-haired, though Valiant's still held the silver sheen of a witch. Twila's silver eyes glowed softly in the grey morning light, marking her as a dragon.

"I wanted to get an early start on my chores," Herja replied. "I'm helping with the harvest today, and couldn't sleep, anyway. Too excited for everyone to arrive."

It had been just over a year since Herja had moved to the Institute, right after she drank from the Silver Springs and was revealed to be a dragon. Typically, children waited until fourteen to join the Institute, but Herja had taken a place here early. As an orphan, she didn't have a family to go home to. So, getting a head start on her studies seemed like a good idea.

Twila smiled warmly at her. "It's a good thing, too. It will give the pigeons a chance to rest," she said with a wink.

Herja took a moment to fight the sense that she had done something wrong. Twila liked to tease about these things, even though it confused Herja. She wished people would just say what they meant to say.

"If I shouldn't be writing to my friends so much—" Herja started, but Valiant waved his hand.

"Twila is in an impish mood this morning and is causing trouble," he said, grinning at his mate. "I caught her putting itching powder in Master Farrow's shoes."

Herja hid her smile beneath her hand. She failed to stifle her giggle at thinking of stoic Farrow jumping around with itchy feet.

Valiant laughed, too. "Don't encourage her!"

"I'm trying not to," Herja said.

Twila smirked. "I don't need any encouragement at all, dear. I was just teasing when I said that about the pigeons. You're welcome to write four or five times a day if you want. Your caretakers at the orphanage aren't coming to the Institute, after all."

Herja nodded once. She had been surprised at how many letters she had received since being here. Letter from Mr. Bryce, the librarian from the village, the other children at the orphanage, and of course, Kaia, Wickham, and Penelope.

"I should get back to work," she said, shifting from foot to foot. "I just have to fix the crates, and then I'll be off for the day."

Twila and Valiant nodded. As they continued, Twila glanced at the crates Herja had already inspected. "Just don't work too hard. Play is important, too."

"Understood," Herja replied seriously.

For some reason, that only made the headmasters giggle as they walked. Herja watched them go, wrapping her arms around her middle.

Despite her excitement for her friends' arrival, Herja wasn't so sure that it was a good thing. Kaia's letters kept describing all the fun they would have. But would it really end up being that way? What if the three other children she had bonded with on the journey to the Silver Springs didn't like her once they spent more time together?

Herja had tried to work on her social skills over this past year, but there wasn't a book she could read and follow. So much of the advice she received boiled down to 'be yourself.'

But what if she wasn't the sort of self that other people liked? Herja had never tried to make friends before. Over this last year, she'd decided she was pretty bad at it.

"And that doesn't help me get my work done," she told herself as she started her chores.

She was just finishing up when the older students who stayed over the summer came out, laughing among themselves. A light rain was drizzling down, making the work cold and miserable. Herja was glad she didn't have to harvest today.

"It's our littlest dragon," one student, a dragon named Gerald, said as the older students drew closer.

Herja scowled. She hated being called 'little.' She might be smaller than them, but she wasn't small for her age. If anything, she was already the same height as the first-years from the last semester. That made her tall.

"What do you want?" she snapped at Gerald, putting her hands on her hips.

"Just being friendly." Gerald's toothy grin set her teeth on edge.

There was just something about him she didn't like.

Gerald looked over the neat stacks of crates she had put together. "Figures they'd give you the easiest job, seeing as you're still a baby," he continued. "I saw you on the obstacle course the other day... even after being here a year, you're still sticking with the baby course."

Herja's hands clenched into fists. "Professor Farrow told me I wasn't allowed on the advanced course yet."

"Because you're just a baby," Gerald said.

Gerald's witch-mate, Charlotte, slapped Gerald's arm. "Leave her alone. You're just jealous that she's already got better marks on the course than you had in your third year."

"I'm done with my work," Herja said loudly. She wasn't sure

whether she liked Charlotte defending her or not... it was probably just more teasing.

Herja walked away, keeping her head up and her shoulders stiff as she did. Being social was so much easier in the letters with Kaia, Wickham, and Penelope she wrote, rather than face-to-face like this.

This thought made her stomach hurt. What if, once they were here, they realized they wanted nothing to do with her? It was much easier to know what to say when she could write it down and rewrite it if it didn't feel right.

She turned her face to the sky. Was Gerald right? Should she have started the more advanced obstacle courses by now? Wouldn't Professor Farrow have told her to advance if she was ready?

Or was the professor holding her back for some reason?

Though she planned to return to the dormitory and change her clothes, Herja changed direction. Why shouldn't she test her strength on the advanced course? She had run the beginner's course so often that she could do it with her eyes closed. So why not try? If she could prove she was ready for it, Professor Farrow might change his mind...

She rounded the large stone building and found the training grounds. Various obstacle courses filled the grounds, except for a large center in the middle where the sparring occurred.

Her heart pounded under her ribs. The beginner's course was a series of hurdles, balance beams, swinging ropes, and walls that the students had to transverse under the eye of the professors. The advanced course wasn't so different. Perhaps a few more swinging ropes, the balance beams might be a little higher.

And all ten feet off the ground.

She placed herself on the starting line and brushed her short, black hair from her face. It was getting damp from the rain, but students were expected to complete the course in all weathers.

"Three, two," Herja crouched into a starting pose. "One!"

She exploded forward, leaping over the first hurdle effortlessly. She skidded around a pole to grab a hanging rope and scaled it, hand over hand. Her teeth gritted together with determination as she bolted up the rope.

If she was going to prove herself to her new friends, she had to be perfect. More than perfect... she had to prove herself to be capable, ready for anything. Her abilities had to overcome the flaws in her personality.

Herja reached the top of the advanced course and scurried along the thin rope bridge, placing her feet carefully. Though she tried to do it without holding onto the railings, she clung to the support ropes to keep her balance. The bridge wobbled and jerked beneath her as though it had a mind of its own.

Lightning flashed overhead as she reached the other side. Herja winced, ducking low to the wooden platform as she counted the seconds by before the crack of thunder followed.

Get back inside, she told herself, then straightened. No! No, she couldn't give up because of a bit of thunder.

Thunder would not hurt her, anyway. It was the lightning that was dangerous. And everything she saw was still far away in the sky. She had three or four hours before the storm's peak hit the Institute.

Rain pelted her, growing colder with each passing moment.

Her lungs heaved for air. It wasn't exertion but fear that made her tremble. Ever since she was young, lightning and thunder terrified Herja. She remembered the gentle smile of a woman sitting by her bedside, telling her everything was all right...

A balance beam was next. It looked narrower up here than it had from the ground. Herja wasn't sure her feet would find purchase with the rain, so she got to her hands and knees, crawling along its length. Lightning flashed. She paused until the thunder rolled and then continued.

What song did Mr. Bryce always sing to the children in the orphanage when they had to deal with thunderstorms?

"Five little speckled frogs sat on a speckled log," she sang as she reached the next platform. Swinging bars were next. She'd have to hold onto them, dangling as she crossed. "Eating the most delicious bugs, yum—"

Lightning.

She held her breath, and her fingers clutched at the wooden platform.

Thunder.

All clear.

"—yum," she finished, trying to ignore the shaking of her voice. "One jumped into the pool, where it was nice and cool."

She grabbed the first of the bars and swung forward, extending her arm to reach the second. The metal was slick and cold, but if she kept moving forward, she wouldn't fall.

"Then there were four green speckled frogs. Glug, glug," she sang, moving her body in beat with the song.

She hurried, her forward momentum taking her from one bar to the next. They swung with her, allowing her to go from one at a time to two.

"Four green and speckled frogs sat on a speckled log, eating the most delicious bugs," she sang louder as lightning flashed. Her words came out as a bellow, drowning out the thunder. "YUM, YUM! ONE JUMPED INTO THE POOL—"

Her friends would appreciate her hard work. They'd be able to see that she did what she was determined to do, and they would help her in her quest for the future.

"—WHERE IT WAS NICE AND COOL—"

Thunder boomed, making her falter.

No! Don't stop. Your friends will be here soon, and then you will have help.

That's what she needed most. Help. Support. Friends who wouldn't tell her she couldn't do this or that, only that she needed to work harder before she got there.

But she had to prove she could help *them*, as well. She had to be strong and brave, and smart. Anybody could learn anything.... And she was going to learn it all, including how to defy the elements and stand in a lightning storm without flinching.

"—THEN THERE WERE THREE GREEN SPECKLED—"

"Herja!"

Her song cut off abruptly as her grip faltered. She looked down, distracted from her forward momentum. Someone was racing toward the obstacle course, but she couldn't see who it was through the sheets of rain.

She reached for the next bar, kicking wildly as her fingers slipped. Her hand closed on nothing, and she plummeted toward the earth as another bolt of lightning cracked the sky open.

CHAPTER

TWO

Penelope's fire-red hair streamed out behind her as she leaned back in the saddle, enjoying the cool air flow around her face. Down in the southern part of Eldavon, where she and her family had been living for the summer, the weather was still hot and sticky. The further north she and Benton traveled, the fresher the air felt.

Her brother tilted slightly to the left in his dragon form as he flew. Penelope grabbed the horn of the saddle and leaned forward again. Benton peered backward with one eye, then tilted his wings downward.

As soon as he landed, Penelope undid the harness that kept her in place and hopped off. She stretched her back, then undid the buckles holding the dragon saddle onto her brother's bulky body.

He shifted smoothly into his human form, shaking out his long sleeves and coat. This he stripped off as he rolled his shoulders.

"That tailwind really helped us along, didn't it?" Benton asked.

Penelope moved through a few stretches as she answered. "Yeah. I wish it hadn't brought that mist with it, though. But I suppose it's a welcome relief after that heat."

She was glad that Benton was sticking with simple conversations. The last few weeks had been filled to the brim with everyone giving her advice and what areas to focus on while training to become part of the Fire Watch upon graduation.

"It's okay to be nervous, you know," Benton said. He was likewise stretching. From experience, Penelope knew he would have to nap before they continued. After all, he was doing all the hard work.

It should have been Benton, her sister Julie, and Da all flying her and Momma to the Institute. Unfortunately, a major fire had broken out, and they were needed to put it out. Benton had been caught in a smoke zone and wasn't back on duty yet, though he was cleared for flying.

Unfortunate for the creatures and people whose homes were in danger, Penelope reflected.

Guilt settled into her stomach. It was almost a relief when Da and Momma told her they wouldn't be able to take her to her first year at the Institute.

It was hard to bite her tongue about her future career choices. She wanted to talk about it, but at the same time, she wasn't ready to. She still had five years at the Institute before picking a job, and even then, if it didn't suit her, she could always change it... right?

"Hey." Benton put his hand on her shoulder, making her jump.

"Don't do that," she snapped.

Benton lifted an eyebrow at her. "Don't do what?"

"Don't scare me."

"I didn't mean to scare you. You're being awfully jumpy, Penelope." Benton's glowing silver eyes, the same as Da's and Julie's and now Penelope's as well narrowed. "Is there something you want to tell me? You were so excited to go to the Silver Springs. What's wrong now? You don't seem to want to go to school."

Penelope bit her lip. It wasn't entirely true. She wanted to go to school, learn and develop these dragon-gifts.

Unfortunately, while she was at school, she would have to focus on the areas of learning that would take her into the military. And she wasn't sure how she would tell her parents that. They'd receive her reports at the end of the year; they'd see that her achievements weren't in line with going into the Fire Watch.

"I'm just nervous about the fire," she finally said, unable to bring herself to tell the truth. "We haven't had anything that big to deal with for a few years. I just hope Da and Julie will be safe."

Benton patted her back. "Don't worry. They know what they're doing, and the Watch has plenty of healers with it right now. There hasn't been a loss of life in over fifty years."

"It can always start up again," Penelope murmured.

Benton didn't seem to hear her as he picked a sleeping bag out of the saddle.

All of the things she was going to have with her at the Institute had been sent ahead, so Benton's load was as light as possible. The only equipment they brought was what they needed to eat and sleep with. Most nights they hadn't even needed to use those, as they landed close to a settlement.

As soon as the locals realized Penelope was going to the Institute, they celebrated with her and gave her and Benton free food and lodging. Of course, she wasn't the only one at some of these places. They had met a few humans going to the Agricultural Trade Academy at their last stop who were receiving the same treatment.

Penelope also grabbed her sleeping bag and rolled it on the ground next to Benton's. Though she wasn't especially tired, staying upright in the saddle was easier when she wasn't exhausted. Best to grab a catnap now.

Unfortunately, she couldn't relax enough to rest. She kept tossing and turning until Benton sighed and pushed himself into a sitting position.

"Sorry," Penelope mumbled, flushing. She hid her face in her arms.

"Something else is bothering you. What's up?"

"Well..." Penelope sighed.

She wasn't sure how to say this. So far, she had told no one about her idea of joining the military instead of the Fire Watch.

She couldn't remember when she hadn't eagerly joined in the

discussions about her future in the Fire Watch. Ever since she could walk, she thought that was her destiny. Trying to figure out how to change that at this point.

The fact was, she was now sure that her gifts would better serve the Kingdom by protecting everyone from outside threats.

"I... I..." Penelope let out a heavy sigh.

As conflicted as she was about this path set before her, as much as she was torn between following her family's dreams for her, her dreams for herself, or choosing what she felt she needed to do... Telling her family was even worse.

Perhaps because part of her still thought she had a chance to change her mind again and get back to what she wanted.

"How did your first year go?" she asked. "And I don't mean for you to be telling me advice or anything like that. I mean, how did it go? I've never been away from home for this long, especially without anyone in the family with me."

Benton put an arm around her. "It was... hard. You had just been born, the unexpected redhead of the family."

He mussed her hair and smirked when she protested, wriggling away from him.

"Mom and Dad had been on parental leave for six months, and they'd have another year at home. I didn't want to go. I cried myself to sleep the first night I was away and had to sneak into Julie's room to sleep at the foot of her bed for a week." Benton shook his head, a nostalgic look on his face. "She must have been annoyed at me but never said a word."

Penelope hugged her knees. She would not have anyone else with her in the Institute. "This isn't helping."

"You're much more stubborn and independent than I was," Benton replied. "But if you end up too lonely, I'll take time off to visit. Promise."

"I'll have my friends," she said slowly. "I'm not really that worried about being lonely. More like... I won't know what to do, or I'll fall behind in class and... all that."

She waved her hand, hoping Benton would understand everything she didn't say. Or rather, everything in accordance with her studies at the Institute. Reports and how well she would perform were indeed stressful, though she was confident in her physical abilities.

"Can you be more specific?" Benton pressed. "Maybe I can help."

"Well... what if I can't change into a dragon?" she blurted the first thing that came to mind.

"That's never happened before."

Penelope folded her arms. "What if it happens to me?"

Benton shook his head. "We all had that fear at one time or another. It won't be a few years before you shift, though... try not to worry about it."

Why did adults all think that was the right thing to say? 'Try not to worry about it' as though her fears were something she tried hard to worry about. The harder she tried not to worry, the worse the worry seemed to get.

"I know that. But... I don't know. Maybe it really is just about the fire." Penelope stood and rolled up her sleeping bag. "I'll go do some exercises and let you rest."

"If you need to talk about anything, let me know, okay?" Benton said as he laid back down.

"Will do."

Penelope wandered off to find a nice, level spot to exercise. But she wasn't in the mood for that, either. She wandered in ever-widening circles until she found a pond, where she crouched near the water and skipped stones across the surface.

They got to the Institute just before dark. Penelope's stomach was so empty and growling that she had no space to be nervous anymore.

"Smells like we're just in time for dinner," Benton said, hurrying Penelope along.

She didn't even have a chance to look at the exterior of the building for the first few rooms they passed other than to note that it was all made of stone.

They arrived in a vast room dotted with round tables throughout the space. While quite a few of the tables were empty, most were occupied by at least one person. She looked around eagerly, searching for familiar faces.

"I don't believe it," a voice shouted from somewhere to the left. "Benton?"

Penelope craned her neck to look around him. Three dragons approached, grinning.

"Cora, Ethan, Jessie!" Benton's face lit up as he bounded over to them. "What are you three doing here?"

"We escorted a handful of the first-years whose guardians couldn't make it," one of them answered. All three sets of glowing silver eyes focused on Penelope. "Is this the sister we heard so much about?"

Penelope shrank back, her shoulders hunching inward.

Benton put his arm around her, his beaming smile getting bigger. "This is Penelope. It's her first year. Penelope, this is Cora, Ethan, and Jessie," he said, gesturing to each.

Penelope memorized the names and faces as she held out her hand. "Pleased to meet you all."

"You are going for the Fire Watch like your brother?" Cora asked. Her hair was twisted up at the nape.

"Um, yeah," Penelope squeaked, fighting her unusual shyness. "I'm looking forward to all the training. I hope that I'll score well."

Benton suddenly steered her in a different direction. "Professor Farrow! I'd like you to meet my sister, Penelope." He bent near her ear. "Farrow is nonbinary. They prefer to be called 'professor' rather than Mx. though."

Professor Farrow. Penelope nodded, though she would have liked to tell Benton that he—and the rest of the family—had told her this information already. She nodded to the professor in greeting. They'd be her teacher this year.

"Welcome," Professor Farrow said to her. Their face was grim and solemn as they looked at her. "I hope you're not a troublemaker like your brother was. I expect you'll keep up with the family legacy for marks, though?"

"I hope so," Penelope replied automatically.

But her heart was sinking. How many people at the Institute would look at her and think of her parents and siblings? They would assume she wanted to be on the Fire Watch too... She had hoped she would see her way more clearly once she was here.

Now, though, she wasn't so sure it would be that easy.

14

THREE

T he wagon jostled back and forth as it bumped over the rutted road. Wickham clutched the carpet bag that held everything he needed to bring to the Institute.

Clothing, bedding, and all other necessities were provided. All Wickham needed to bring were those belongings that would help him feel more comfortable for the three months until winter break.

Donnelly and Rhett, his eleven-year-old brothers, raced to either side of the wagon, trying to 'beat' it to whatever finish line they had decided. Three-year-old Tara was, thankfully, fast asleep next to Wickham, her head on his shoulder. Normally, she'd be running around with them.

Even though Wickham had been trying to do as Mother and Father suggested and not interfere with his brothers' play unless he thought they were putting themselves in danger, it was hard. He didn't like the idea of them running alongside these heavy wagons with their spinning wheels and the heavy hooves of the horses tramping and stamping along the hard-packed earth.

If Tara were awake, she would want to run around, too. And she was still tiny enough that she didn't always understand what 'stay away from the wagons' meant. The twins at least kept a reasonable distance from them.

Father jogged up to the end of the wagon and pulled himself in. His cheeks were flushed, eyes bright, with a beaming smile on his face.

"Are you all right?" Wickham asked, noting how heavily his father was breathing.

"Fine," Father said, waving his hand. The attempt to seem casual was marred by a coughing fit.

Wickham found the family bag and dug into it, looking for the peppermint camphor they had brought along for Father's persistent cough. He had almost recovered from the disease he'd caught last year, but it would take some time for him to build up his strength again.

"Thank you," Father said, accepting the peppermint camphor.

It was a waxy substance that usually would melt easily, but it was mixed in with a gelatin mixture that kept the properties to ease a person's lungs while making it easier to transport. This batch was one that Wickham had made himself just before they left.

"You look pensive," Father noted, offering Wickham a hand. "You're about to twist that handle right off the bag."

Wickham reluctantly handed it over. "I'm just worried that we'll be late, is all. We were supposed to be there by now."

Father hummed and looked up at the sky. "And?"

"And... I'm worried how hard this will be on you," Wickham admitted. "I'm happy everyone could get the time to come with me, but... are you sure that it will not set back your recovery?"

"Wick, we've had this discussion before."

Wickham frowned. "We have, but that was before; now it's now, and we have been traveling for so long."

"And we're almost there. No point in turning around now before we can see you settled." Father kissed the top of his head and tugged lightly on the end of Wickham's silvery braid. "You worry too much about me, Wick. Much too much."

Wickham huffed. "I do not. I worry just enough. You don't worry enough."

"Wickham. It's a parent's job to make sure their child doesn't have that weight on their shoulders," Father shook his head.

"That doesn't help me feel better."

"What I mean is that your mother and I discussed this in great detail. We know what we'll do if I have a relapse. We also decided that I was well enough to take part. It's not as though riding in a wagon is any harder on me than going back to work."

Wickham opened his mouth, then closed it again. He folded his arms, scowling. "You could have talked to me about it."

"Wick—"

"No, don't 'Wick' me in that tone." Wickham slumped backward. He kept his voice low so as not to wake Tara, but it was difficult. Wick sounded like he was sulking, which wasn't what he wanted to convey. He didn't want Father to think he was sulking about this. "What I mean is, you know that I'm worried. You could have told me why you think you're well enough for this."

Father sighed. "We did talk about it."

It was true... on the other hand, Wickham never felt like they took his concerns seriously. "I... I'm sorry for my tone."

"I understand. You have a big heart, Wick. And you always want to help others... this last year was hard, especially on you and Mother."

Wickham ducked his head. "It just seems like as soon as you got better enough to bring Tara back home, I have to leave. I will miss you all... and I still don't want to go. I don't understand why I can't just keep learning from the herbalist."

Father brushed his hair from his face. "That's the real reason, then?"

Wickham hesitated. It was essential to be at the Institute. All the reasons passed through his mind: to be around other witches, to meet his Dragon match—although that wouldn't be decided until the end of next year—to learn from the professors who had trained to teach young children and also had years of experience, to see his friends again...

Father adjusted his seat on the wagon to get closer to Wickham. He put an arm around him. Wickham leaned into Father's side.

"You just got better, and Tara just got home," Wickham repeated. "I don't want to leave, not now. If I could just defer for one year, I'd still work with Kassandra with the herbs, and then I'd just be a year older when I graduate."

"You have already learned about every herb in Kassandra's garden, from how to grow them to what they do."

Wickham ground his teeth. "That's not the point."

He knew that the basis of herbs and plants he already knew would greatly help him. But he already knew he wanted to be a healer. Why shouldn't he stay home and learn how to specialize in healing rather than go to school so far away and learn about everything else?

"I think," Father said, his tone gentle, "the point is that you have always thought you needed to take care of your younger siblings. And your parents, too."

Wickham had to admit that was true. He was the oldest. It was his responsibility to make sure that the younger children behaved themselves and to take as much burden off his parents as possible. They both worked long and hard hours.

Sure, they had Crown-appointed childcare in the town that Tara adored going to, and the twins were in basics school for another two years until they graduated. But...

"If I didn't need to be there, I wouldn't feel so insistent," Wickham said, trying it at a different angle. "Maybe it's my magic telling me I need to stay home."

He already knew it was a hopeless argument. His parents hadn't listened to him so far; why would they start now?

"It's because your mother nearly died with the twins," Father replied. "You were so young, and too much of our attention went to them because they were so tiny and frail... I'm sorry that I made you feel like all this is your responsibility, Wick. But you must learn how to live your own life and not dedicate everything to this family."

"Why is looking after my family a bad thing?"

"It's not. But what you want to do goes beyond looking after your family. Defer one year, and next year won't be easier." Father hugged him. "I love you. I love that you have such a big heart. But your entire existence can't be wrapped up in our little village with our family... the twins and Tara are growing up. They'll move away, eventually. Will you put off going to the Institute until they're gone?"

"Is that so bad?"

Father smiled at him, and Wickham couldn't help but smile back.

"I see it!" Donnelly shouted suddenly.

He came racing around the back of the wagon, too close to the wheel. He stumbled, and Wickham jumped to catch him, but Father was there first. He pulled Donnelly away from the wheel and helped to steady him.

Tara lifted her head with a whining noise. Wickham was torn between staying with her and seeing how Donnelly was... but if he left, Tara might try to stumble after him, and she'd get hurt. Father, and now Mother and Rhett, were all with Donnelly.

Maybe this is what Father means, Wickham thought doubtfully that *I'm needed more at the Institute than at home.*

He sighed as Tara put her head back down, moving her thumb into her mouth. Usually, Wickham would attempt to move that thumb out of her mouth, but today it seemed like too much of a fight.

He had accepted that he would be at the Institute this year. What brought on this sudden argument was how Father's coughing reminded him of the situation... when moments before, he had been thinking only of how excited he was to see his friends again.

The wagon train rolled up to the Institute, but Wickham kept his eyes on the ground, not looking at the massive, castle-like building.

"Everyone gather around," Mother called. She pulled something from the wagon, and everyone knelt in a circle on the grass as the wagon master was greeted by a handful of people wearing dark blue uniforms.

Wickham chewed his bottom lip, head still bowed.

"Wick, we know this is a hard time for you," Mother said, "so we decided to get you this gift."

She pushed the package she had taken from the wagon toward him.

Wickham looked up at last, confused. The twins looked on eagerly while Tara started whining about not getting a present herself. Wickham let Father deal with her as he slowly untied the ribbon, holding the package shut.

The paper fell away, revealing a square box. It was divided into sections, and the top could detach from the bottom. As he looked closer at it, Wickham realized it was a combination of a growing and storage box. The top could be used separately to plant herbs in, while the bottom was stocked full of everything he could use.

Small burlap sacks sat on top of the dried herbs. Mint. Chamomile. Garlic. Many more. Everything he needed to grow his own small herb garden.

"This is... perfect," he choked as his throat swelled with emotion.

Mother and Father beamed at him. Wickham carefully put the herb box together and hugged it to his chest. He couldn't say more; the lump in his throat was too big. But it seemed like his parents understood. The twins looked slightly bored, but he didn't expect them to realize how important this was.

The people in blue uniforms approached the family. Wickham got to his feet awkwardly to face them.

"Welcome to the Institute," the leader said with a slight bow. "Would you like us to take your things to the dormitory?"

Wickham glanced at his parents. This was it. They were already here. Why should he still feel like he needed to turn back?

It was only for three months, after all... and he was looking forward to his friends.

Wickham straightened his shoulders. "Yes, please. I would be very grateful for that."

The uniformed people bowed again, and Wickham awkwardly bowed back. He wasn't used to this sort of treatment.

"There will be a welcome speech in the dining hall in half an hour," the leader said. "In the meantime, feel free to look around."

"Let's go see the pond!" Donnelly instantly said excitedly. "Maybe there are sharks!"

Rhett rolled his eyes. "Sharks only live in lakes."

Wickham had to laugh. "Sharks are in the ocean. Not ponds or lakes. But we have to go see the pond, anyway."

As the family headed toward the small, blue pond, some tension eased from Wickham's shoulders. This was where he needed to be, even if he didn't want to admit it... and he was eager to see Kaia, Penelope, and Herja again.

FOUR

K aia scribbled happily in her journal, detailing everything she could see out her window... well, everything she could get down before they passed it, at least. She'd picked up journalling over the past year and was eager to improve her skills.

"You're missing the first sight of the Institute, dearest," Mama said. Her silvery hair, pin-straight and pulled into a bun, glinted in the afternoon sunlight.

Kaia finished her sentence and looked out the window again. She didn't see any sign of the Institute yet, just fields of flowing golden wheat. Or were those canola flowers?

Papa, whose wild curls were exactly the same as Kaia's, save for the color, laughed as he shook his head. "Let the girl write, Liv. If it makes her happy, it makes her happy."

"I'm not saying Kaia shouldn't write," Mama protested. "Just that she's been talking so much seeing the Institute for the first time, and we'll be there soon."

Kaia huffed. She set her journal aside and grabbed hold of the bar just below the window to lean out. The vast fields were so beautiful that they took her breath away, especially with the mountains in the far distance. She would enjoy waking up every morning to see such a beautiful sight.

"I don't see it," she complained, withdrawing back into the carriage.

"See? We're not close yet."

Mama frowned at the map she had laid out on her lap. "I was certain we were farther along."

As Mama and Papa went over the map, Kaia turned her attention to the carriage's other occupant. Adina was also a witch, as Kaia was. She slumped in her seat, arms folded tightly. The dour expression on her face made Kaia want to ignore her.

But, if Kaia was going to be leaving for the Institute and her parents hadn't been able to come along, she would be sulky, too.

Maybe there was a way for Kaia to cheer her up. "How are you doing, Adina?"

"I'm all right."

"You seem to be quiet today," Kaia pressed. "Would you like to have a little break from the carriage?"

Adina shook her head. "I'm just tired from all the traveling. I would rather just get to the Institute as quickly as possible."

"It has been a long journey," Kaia agreed in sympathy. "It becomes quite tedious to sit for hours upon hours every day. That's why I like to write in my journal while we travel."

"If I look at anything with words, my head spins, and I feel like I'm going to vomit," Adina replied sadly.

Kaia flinched. "I'm sorry. I didn't know."

Adina shrugged.

"I should have asked earlier," Kaia continued. "If I had known, I could have been reading aloud to you. It would help the time pass a little faster, at least."

Adina shrugged again and looked out the window.

She didn't seem to want to talk. Kaia cast her mind for anything that might bring Adina out of her shell, then leaned back in her seat. Maybe Adina just wanted to be alone with her thoughts.

Kaia had spent almost the entire summer near Adina at the palace. Both their parents were working hard in the King's wake of Odentia, a kingdom next to theirs, demanding that Eldavon allow their thirteen-year-olds to drink from the Silver Springs to gain magic.

Or at least, their thirteen-year-olds from nobility. The Odentian king had made it very clear he believed the 'lower classes' shouldn't be allowed to same opportunities, which Kaia thought was just stupid. The nobility wasn't guaranteed to have magic among them just because they were nobles.

But then, Kaia had learned that Odentia differed significantly from Eldavon. Their king had been king since he was a baby and was only king because his father was king... It was strange, considering that Eldavon had two kings and two queens who were all elected to the position.

It had been an interesting summer, however. Kaia had learned a lot about how the palace worked. More importantly, how each king and queen worked. The dragon King Lantos had a much more unique style for his meetings than the human King Diesel, and Queen Johanna, as a witch, held her court differently from the human Queen Charlize.

Queen Charlize was the one who allowed Kaia to sit in on discussions more than the other three. Kaia understood, as there were certain things a child shouldn't be involved in, but she still felt a special bond with the human queen.

Staying at the palace had undoubtedly given her a much deeper understanding of how the Crown functioned and the amount of work the kings and queens put in to ensure everyone in the Kingdom was taken care of.

She looked forward to detailing everything to Herja in particular since Herja wanted to be Queen one day.

The carriage came to a stop, and moments later, the door was opened by the coachman. He smiled at them apologetically. "One horse threw a shoe, and it hit another. We must make sure they're all right before we continue."

Kaia eagerly climbed from the carriage. Her back ached with all the sitting she had been doing these past few weeks.

As her parents and Adina followed, Kaia skimmed the path ahead.

She stifled an excited shout as she caught sight of the building ahead of them.

"There it is!" she cried, pointing, unable to tamp down her enthusiasm entirely.

Mama, Papa, and Adina gathered around. The Institute was closer than Kaia had thought, but she understood why she hadn't seen it before, as the carriage had been in a slight dip. As she looked at the building, her chest warmed with excitement.

"It's beautiful," she sighed.

It was built in the style of a cathedral palace, which made sense as it had once been a palace. Towers spiraled upwards at each corner, while the middle was an enormous glass dome that twinkled with a rainbow of color. That had to be the atrium.

Kaia bounced up and down, her arms folded tightly across her chest to stop it from bouncing, too... puberty had hit her hard this past year, and it seemed she was going to take after her mother as far as proportions go. Short and wide. It wouldn't bother Kaia so much, except boys were looking at her differently now.

"It's the Institute," Adina said, sounding listless.

Kaia extended a hand to her. "Why don't we start walking? It will be a welcome change to sitting in the carriage."

Adina glanced at Mama and Papa.

"You girls go ahead," Mama said, nodding.

Adina shrugged and took Kaia's hand. They walked toward the Institute, albeit Adina quickly ended up with a fast pace Kaia wasn't entirely happy with.

"It's exciting to start our education in magic, isn't it?" Kaia asked after some time.

Adina shook her head. "I can't be excited about anything right now."

"But... I thought you'd be happy since your parents were just elected to replace King Diesel and Queen Charlize."

Adina scowled. "I'm not happy at all. Why would I be happy that King Diesel is dying?"

Kaia winced. "He's not dying. He's just sick."

"He's *dying*. The election was held because of it. And my parents are going to be King and Queen, and all my older siblings will go to work in the government." Adina's voice was a growl.

"I... don't understand. Why is that a problem?"

"I don't want to do that. I didn't want to be a witch. I wanted to study childcare, and now...."

Adina released Kaia's hand and sped up even more.

Kaia struggled to keep up with her. She hadn't thought of all that sort of stuff, though she had known that Adina didn't want to be a witch. She'd felt Adina had accepted it, in any case. But why did her other siblings being in government mean that Adina needed to be as well?

"Everything was more chaotic because the transition is still happening," Kaia said, panting. "They would have come with you to the Institute if they could have."

Adina turned toward her, tears glinting in her eyes. "I didn't want them to come!" she yelled. "Don't you see? I told them not to come. I told them I didn't want them to be here. I told them to stay behind because the Kingdom needs them!"

Kaia flinched again. The sudden stop had left her even more breathless than their fast pace.

"I don't want to be a witch. I don't want to have to serve the Kingdom," Adina continued. Her hands were clenched into fists, and she breathed heavier. "I want to be *me*. I don't even know who the girl in the mirror is anymore."

"Adina—"

"You can't understand. You wanted this. You wanted it all!" Adina spread her arms wide and shook her head. "I don't. I just wanted to have a simple life. To be able to choose a simple path. Now everyone is constantly asking me what career I'm going to pursue. As if I have any idea!"

Kaia tried to think of what to say. "There are lots of options."

"And all of them are ones that witches have," Adina shot back. "Do they have childcare courses here? No! Because witches are supposed to learn magic and then use magic for the good of the Kingdom."

"Don't you want to help the Kingdom?" Kaia asked, stunned.

Adina's eyes overflowed. "Of course I do. I want to help. But I want to help with children. I don't want to have to choose anything more specific than that. Fourteen is too young to decide what you will do for the rest of your life. Humans can go back to school. Witches, once you graduate—"

"You can go back to school, too," Kaia interrupted. She stepped closer to the other girl. "Once you graduate from the Institute, you can look at any of the other schools and train for childcare."

Adina frowned. "Everyone will think it's a waste of my magic."

"No, they won't. Just think about how much other young witches who feel the same way would like to have a witch teacher in school. Or children who are going to go to the Silver Springs, needing to have a first-hand account of what it's like? After all, did you have anyone to talk to before you went?"

Adina chewed her lip. "My family. They all went to the Silver Springs, too."

"And you're the only witch in the family," Kaia nodded. "So if you had a witch as a tutor or the like, you would better understand what the future is like. Too often, we assume that everyone knows what it means, but we don't... even me, and my mother is a witch."

Adina's shoulders slowly relaxed as she wiped her eyes. "I suppose. But there are so few witches...."

Kaia hugged her tightly. "Listen. I know it's hard, but it's going to be okay. You have to forge your own path to help the Kingdom. And as for your parents being the new king and queen... well, I suppose that means you'll be under more scrutiny, but that doesn't mean you shouldn't follow your dreams."

Adina hid her face in Kaia's shoulder. "It just feels so impossible."

Feeling rather motherly, Kaia patted Adina's silver hair. "I know it does. But the important thing is not to let yourself break the eggs before they hatch."

"What?" Adina pulled away. She giggled. "That's not how that saying goes!"

"Why not? I can make up my own sayings," Kaia replied. She winked. "I follow my own dreams, you see."

Adina laughed louder this time. "Are you saying your dream is to make up new sayings?"

"It might be," Kaia hedged.

Truthfully, she had no clue what her future career would be. But she had time to figure that out. For now, she took hold of Adina's hand again and started for the Institute. She was glad she'd managed to get the other girl to smile again.

CHAPTER
FIVE

"Kaia!" Wickham leaped out of his seat to rush to her, hugging her tightly. He even lifted her off her feet; he was so excited to see her.

Kaia made an 'oof' noise and laughed. "Wick! You made it before I did."

Wickham released her and stepped back to grin at her. "I only got in yesterday; I haven't had time to see anything yet. What about you?"

"Just an hour ago," Kaia replied. "I thought we would miss orientation, but we made it."

The girl standing beside her looked on with a look of mild interest. She had silver hair, just as Wickham and Kaia did. Wickham recognized her from the journey to the Silver Springs, but he couldn't remember her name.

"Hi, I'm Wickham," he said, offering his hand.

"Adina."

They shook, and Wickham led them to a table where other first-year witch students sat. "This is Icarus, Jalene, and Lena. And this is Kaia and Adina."

"I know you," Jalene said as she propped her elbows on the table.

"You're Abigail and Sydney's daughter, aren't you? So... you're like a princess now, right?"

Adina scowled. Wickham looked at them, surprised. He had heard of the changes that were happening with the in human king and queen but hadn't paid much attention to it all. After all, the king and queen didn't seem to impact his little village. Why should he pay attention when there was so much more that he had to worry about?

"I see Pen!" Kaia grabbed Wickham's arm and pulled. "Let's go say hi."

Wickham was glad to follow along with her. Now that Kaia had pointed her out, he easily spied Penelope's fire-red hair. A grin blossomed over his face as he and Kaia ran up to her. She'd grown in the last year; during the trip to the Silver Springs, he'd been taller than Penelope. Now, she was at least an inch taller than he was.

Kaia and Penelope chattered to each other both at once, and Wickham was happy enough to stand by and answer questions directed at him.

"I can't wait to get started," Kaia gushed as she grinned at the two of them. "We're going to have such a wonderful time together; I can just feel it! Oh, Wick! How is your father doing? I know you were worried about him."

Wickham sighed. "He's... recovered mostly. I'm still worried, but he and Mother both keep telling me not to worry."

Kaia patted his shoulder. "I'm sure he's fine, then."

"I hope so."

Penelope waved her hand at them. "Shh! Headmasters Twila and Valiant have just arrived."

The three of them quickly found spots at a table, though Wickham's seat was facing away from the high podium where the two headmasters ascended. Both stood at the podium, Headmaster Valiant with his silvery hair and Headmaster Twila with her silver eyes.

Wickham straightened in his seat and twisted around as he was. He gripped the back of his chair with both hands, his heart pounding faster than he thought it would... He found himself being excited, which he hadn't expected.

"Greetings, new students and old," Headmaster Valiant said, spreading his hands toward them. "A new year, new challenges, and new friends await you all. I hope you will find your footing quickly. Now, a few bits of administration before we begin our meal."

There were a few audible groans in the crowd, but Wickham ignored them.

"First, to those who don't know, the Institute has dozens of pigeons and messengers that can take letters home to your families. Pigeons are meant to be for emergency usage, but if you feel you have such an emergency, please let Headmaster Twila or I know."

Headmaster Twila nodded and took over, "For the new students, you have been assigned beds in the dormitories; this will be your space for the next five years, and you may decorate within the space as you would like. Anything in common spaces must be discussed and agreed on by all your roommates."

"Each dormitory has a house rector responsible for disputes, cleanliness, and safety. The name of your rector will be listed on your doors. Do not hesitate to go to them for any problem." Headmaster Valiant paused as he looked over the faces. "You have all been part of orientation, correct?"

"Yes," Kaia said behind Wickham. "I wish we could have seen more, though."

She didn't speak loud enough for Headmaster Valiant to hear, but Wickham turned around. "Penelope and I can show you around after dinner. I wanted to be able to explore a bit more, too. Especially the medical wing."

Maybe, if he weren't too busy with his studies, he could volunteer there for a little while.

The headmasters continued to tell everyone the basics of what sort of behavior and responsibilities were expected of the students, but Wickham tuned it out. His stomach was rumbling, and he quickly became impatient.

Other students were getting more fidgety as well, and finally, the two headmasters declared that the food would be served.

Dozens of people came into the hall, moving from table to table wearing crisp black and white uniforms. They wheeled silver carts ahead of them, filled to the brink with all sorts of food. Wickham's mouth watered as one of them stopped by their table.

After the three of them had been served food, they dug in. Wickham closed his eyes, savoring the taste of this food. It was one thing he was super happy about—since they didn't have access to these spices in the village.

"So, where should we start the tour?" Penelope said after some time. "Kaia, do you know how to find your dorm?"

Kaia nodded. "Let's start with the library. I would love to see all their books!"

THE LIBRARY WAS FILLED to the brink. Not only books but also comfortable chairs to sit next to fireplaces, desks to work at, and some shelves with a fantastic array of artifacts that had been carefully preserved and now were on display.

Kaia hardly noticed any of it. As soon as they walked in, she remembered how last year Herja had that magical bag she'd used to carry a dozen books up the side of the mountain.

"I didn't see Herja at the dinning hall," she said. "I know she's here at the Institute; we've been keeping in touch."

Penelope shrugged. "I figured since she already knows the rules and regulations here, she decided to take dinner in her dorm."

Wickham frowned. "Wouldn't she have the same dorm as you? You're both first-year dragons."

A wrinkle formed between Penelope's eyebrows. "I guess. I haven't seen her; I didn't think about us being in the same dorm... maybe she's in the second year?"

"No, she's not," Kaia folded her arms, shivering. "In her last letter to me, she complained that even though she sat in on all the lectures for first years last year, she isn't being put to the second year. You don't think something is wrong, do you?"

"We could ask Headmaster Twila," Wickham offered.

Penelope glanced around and lowered her voice. "You don't think she lied, do you? Pretending to be here at the Institute but really going off and doing her own thing?"

"No way," Kaia said.

"How would you know?"

"Because I know." Kaia lifted her chin stubbornly. "Herja wouldn't do that. She has to be here somewhere. Let's check your dorm."

Penelope led the way. The stone corridors grew narrower until they were just wide enough for four people to walk side-by-side. The dorm rooms were in the high northern tower, and Kaia was surprised that both witches and dragons lived in the same area. Rather than being divided up by what magic they held, they were divided by what year they were in.

The common room was round and had four doors leading from it. Penelope showed Wickham and Kaia her room. Adina sat on one of the beds, and looked up in surprise.

"Oh, hello," Penelope greeted. "I'm Pen—your roommate. And these are my friends—"

"We know Adina already," Kaia said. She approached the other witch. "How are you doing?"

"Tired after that fantastic meal," Adina said with a brief smile.

"We won't keep you, then," Penelope said.

Kaia moved to the third bed in the room. The name *Lena* was etched into the trunk that sat at the end.

Wickham's roommates were Icarus and Nolen. Kaia's were Jalene and Odele. They couldn't enter the other rooms without permission, and knocking gave no answer.

So where was Herja?

PENELOPE COULD SEE both Kaia and Wickham's nervousness increase as they searched every classroom on the first level.

"I don't think it's that big of a deal," Penelope complained, tailing after them. "Herja is independent. She'll be at the first day of classes, I'm sure of it. Did either of you actually arrange to see her during orientation?"

Wickham closed the classroom door he'd been peering into and turned to Penelope to put his hands on his hips. "It's reasonable to expect us to see our friend, Penelope. I just don't know where she could be."

Penelope rolled her shoulders, trying to relieve the tension, then had a thought. "Come with me."

She turned on her heel and marched away. Kaia and Wickham both questioned her as she walked, sounding increasingly upset.

"The floor rector is there for our help, right?" Penelope asked them impatiently.

"Uh... I guess?" Wickham said.

"We'll ask him then—er. Actually, I don't know their pronouns. Our floor rector is named Alex," she added as she took the stairs toward the dorms again. "They're on the floor above ours. If they don't know where Herja is, it's a matter for the teachers to get involved."

Penelope turned her head slightly, hearing Kaia starting to pant. She slowed her pace, making it more comfortable for her friend.

They reached the rector's common room soon enough. Penelope glanced over at the fifth-year witches and dragons and cleared her throat.

"Excuse me; we're looking for our floor rector, Alex."

A willowy dragon rose to their feet and headed over. They were an androgynous figure with chin-length hair and soft face that was both feminine and masculine.

"I'm Alex. Penelope, Wickham, and Kaia, right? I stopped into your common room to introduce myself earlier. Pronouns are he or them," he added with a knowing smile.

Penelope blushed. Her question must have been clear on her face. "Er... thank you. I apologize if I made you uncomfortable."

"It's no problem. Now, what can I do for you?"

"We're looking for a girl on our floor," Kaia said. "Herja?"

One of the other dragons laughed. "That little know-it-all is your friend? I'm sorry."

Penelope frowned at the dragon.

Alex also frowned but shook his head. "Ignore Gerald. He's just... Gerald. Now. Herja's in the medical wing. She had an accident on the obstacle course a few days ago."

"Oh no!" Kaia gasped, grabbing Penelope's arm. "Is she okay?"

"She will be," Alex reassured them. "You're free to go visit."

"Thank you," Penelope said.

She quickly led the other two from the room. It was another rather long walk to the medical wing. Relief washed over her as soon as she saw Herja sitting in bed, reading. Kaia and Wickham rushed over, but Penelope hung back. She didn't want to seem overeager, after all.

"We were looking everywhere for you," Kaia exclaimed.

Herja looked a little uncomfortable as Kaia hugged her. "Sorry?"

"We didn't look everywhere," Penelope said. She sat on the edge of Herja's bed. "What happened?"

"Twisted my ankle pretty bad. I was doing the obstacle course in the rain," Herja said, then grimaced. "It was stupid."

"You're going to be all right," Wickham said. He had picked up the chart at the foot of Herja's bed and flipped through it. "Ah, willow tea. Good, that should help with the pain."

Penelope took the chart and put it back. "You're not allowed to look at that."

Wickham opened his mouth, then closed it again. He moved up to sit beside Herja on the opposite side of Kaia. "All right, then. Tell us everything."

"Everything about...?" Herja arched a single eyebrow.

"Everything," Kaia exclaimed. "Leave nothing out!"

Penelope and Herja shared a look. Penelope had to roll her eyes slightly, but she smiled. The four of them were back together. Good. This year would be great, so long as she kept her friends around.

CHAPTER
SIX

Herja rolled her ankle in circles, mindful not to overextend it. She had been deemed fully fit to join the first day of classes with the other first-year dragons. There were only six of them in total. Herja knew there wouldn't be many of them, but she hadn't paid enough attention during the trip from the Silver Springs to see how many there were.

Just under one-third of the population ended up as dragons or witches, and then of that number, it was split evenly between dragons and witches.

Still, six seemed like a pitifully small number of students.

Herja shook her head as Penelope rushed in, breathing hard. Her face was flushed with sleep still, and there was a tiny bit of sleep sand in the corner of her eye.

"You're almost late," Herja told her under her breath.

Penelope plopped into the chair next to her. "I got lost."

Herja shook her head, then slid a paper across the table. "I made maps for you, Kaia, and Wickham. I gave Kaia and Wickham theirs at breakfast... thought you'd be there," she added, a note of disproval in her voice.

"I missed the wake-up call."

Herja couldn't help but think that Penelope was going to have to put in a lot more effort than she was currently showing if she was going to be successful at this.

"Besides," Penelope continued, looking around. "You're the only one here. Are you sure this is the right room?"

Herja bristled, but before she could snap back that she was sure, sure, the door opened. Professor Farrow, dressed in a deep blue uniform, walked in. Students wouldn't receive their uniforms until after the matching ceremony.

Herja's stomach twisted, but she pushed it aside. The ceremony wouldn't happen until the end of next year. No point in worrying about it now. She wished that she could have a uniform like that now, though. It would be easier than figuring out what she would wear every morning.

"Herja, Penelope," Professor Farrow greeted with a somber nod to both of them.

"Good morning, Professor," Herja said in a clipped tone. She still hadn't forgiven them for startling her on the obstacle course, even if they caught her before she hit the ground.

"Professor," Penelope nodded toward them. "I'm looking forward to starting classes. Actually, I'm most excited about the physical training. I've been practicing, but it'll be good to better understand where I need to focus my efforts."

The four other students trailed into the room, looking a little nervous.

"Nolen, Xena, Odele, Vera," Professor Farrow greeted them. "Please find seats for yourselves; then we will go around and introduce ourselves, our pronouns, and one thing you hope to learn this year."

The students quickly found seats. Nolen sat next to Herja, and Herja wished she had taken a seat at the edge of the room rather than right in the middle. She tried to ignore the nerves bubbling in her stomach.

"I'll start," Professor Farrow said, sitting on a desk. "I'm Professor Farrow and use they/them pronouns. You may call me Farrow, Professor, or Professor Farrow. Mx. will work in a pinch, but I prefer

Professor or just Farrow. I hope to learn five unfamiliar words this year, so I expect you each to scour the dictionary and come up with a new one every day until you find one I haven't heard before."

They paused a moment, and their gaze fixed on Herja. "And only one," he added.

Herja ducked her head, flushing.

"Xena?" Professor Farrow continued.

"Um... I'm Xena, and use he/him pronouns," the shy-looking dragon said. "I want to learn how to swim. Better. Because I know how to swim a little but not much."

Herja chewed her lip. She hadn't put in a lot of work for swimming... should she work on that?

"Vera, she/her. And I want to learn how to climb!" the dark-haired girl jumped to her feet and mimicked climbing.

I know how to do that pretty good. Herja thought.

"I'm Odele, and use she/her pronouns," the next person said. She sat straight up, staring ahead with a deadly serious expression. "This year, I hope to learn not one thing in particular but have a holistic improvement in my abilities."

"Nolen. He/him. Improved balance."

Herja started a little at how quickly Nolen had passed over his introduction. That meant it was her now. Her cheeks flushed. How was she supposed to do this? Even though she'd sat through this class before, her tongue suddenly felt too fat for her mouth even though she had these examples.

"Herja," she finally managed. "She/her. I want to learn... everything."

She glanced at her notebook, clenching her hands in her lap.

Luckily, Penelope took over without so much as needing a prompt. "I'm Penelope, and I use she/her pronouns, though I usually don't mind being referred to as 'them.' And what I want to learn is what areas I need to focus on so I can join the military upon graduation."

Herja's head jerked up. She nearly protested right there, and only embarrassment for her previous stammering stopped her. She had been confident that Penelope wanted to join the Fire Watch. Wasn't that all she talked about on their journey to the Silver Springs?

"The military?" Professor Farrow repeated.

"Yes, Professor."

"Hmm. Well, at this point, your education will be equal across all areas that you need for traditional dragon careers. However, it depends on what area of the military you are hoping to get into. We can meet with Headmaster Twila to discuss it in more detail."

Penelope nodded once, a determined look on her face. "Thank you, Professor."

Herja picked up her pencil and doodled in her notebook as Professor Farrow went back to Xena to explain how much time they would spend in the water.

What made Penelope so interested in the military? Eldavon was a peaceful Kingdom, and they rarely had any troubles from outside kingdoms. She knew that some of the other kingdoms ended up fighting each other, but it had been years since there had been any threats to Eldavon.

Except for last year... Herja glanced from the corner of her eye at Penelope. Was her change of heart because of the Odentian warriors that had attempted to kidnap the witches and dragons from the Silver Springs?

In any case, Herja would not question her. Penelope knew what she wanted, just as Herja did.

"Herja?" Professor Farrow said, breaking into her thoughts.

Herja put her pencil down. "Yes, Professor?"

"I was asking if there was anything more specific you wanted to learn about, and failing that, what 'everything' means to you."

Herja felt her cheeks warming again. Why did everyone have to look at her? Why did Professor Farrow have to bring so much attention to her? She straightened. "Everything means I want to ensure I'm the best I can be at every aspect of training. I have to be the best because I intend to be the queen one day."

Nolen and Odele stifled laughter, and Herja's cheeks burned even hotter. What were they laughing for? Someone had to have the job.

Professor Farrow nodded, standing. "Thank you. Now. Does anyone know what this year's training will look like?"

HERJA'S HAND shot up into the air and nearly clipped Penelope's chin. She jerked away from the other girl narrowing her eyes. Herja ignored her disapproval.

Professor Farrow turned a stern look on Herja, but their lips still twitched like they found the situation amusing. "Herja, since you have been an observer for a year already, I would like to give the other students a chance to answer questions."

She dropped her hand, her usually pale skin almost the same shade as Penelope's hair.

Odele's hand rose.

"Yes, Odele?" Professor Farrow prompted.

"I understand that the first year is mostly to ensure that the Institute has a basis for our physical capabilities as well as ensuring the students are more or less on the same physical standpoint. Is this correct?" she asked, sounding stiff.

Penelope rested her elbows on the table. If that's all there was to it, why were they in a classroom?"

"That is a major focus, yes," Professor Farrow. "However, a dragon's training isn't just about their physical abilities. We also train in first aid, crowd management, and various other tasks. As I said, the first year is mostly focused on the physical. We will train in various forms of exertion, but also meditation. And we will study the terrain, the various muscle groups, proper nutrition, and how to avoid and care for injuries."

Penelope bit back the desire to say she already knew all of that. She came from a family of nearly all dragons, after all. She had been participating in daily exercises and listening to her siblings recite major muscle groups for years.

40

We all have new things to learn, though, she reminded herself. She picked up her pencil to be ready to take notes.

"The first thing we need to learn is how our bodies work." Professor Farrow unfurled a large piece of paper and tacked it to the wall. It showed the image of a skeleton next to another of a person made of muscles and a third made of red and blue lines. "Who can tell me what this is?"

Odele and Herja shot up their hands, but Herja dropped hers again.

"The study of the body made by the witch-queen Daisy twenty years ago," Odele rattled off before Professor Farrow called on her. "She used her specialized magic to capture images of what the body looked like inside. The first is the skeletal structure, section the major muscle groups, and the third is the vein and artery systems."

Professor nodded. "Yes, you are correct. Next time, however, wait until I call on you before you answer my question."

Penelope glanced across Herja and Nolen at Odele. Odele was staring back at Professor Farrow with an almost challenging look, unlike the way Herja had ducked her head and flushed.

This was going to be interesting for sure... and not in a good way, Penelope was sure.

She raised her hand. Maybe she could head this off.

"Yes, Penelope?" Professor Farrow asked.

"I was just going to say I learned about this from my older siblings. I was just wondering if Nolen, Vera, and Xena had also had the opportunity."

Professor Farrow arched an eyebrow but nodded. "Have you?" they asked the three other students.

Nolen cleared his throat. "Odele told me."

Xena scratched his head, looking somewhat embarrassed. He finally shook his head, looking down.

"Nope," Vera chirped.

"Very well," Professor Farrow said. "Then I will have you all sit for the test, and if you four pass, then Xena and Vera will have tutoring to catch up while we get started on the next section. Please put your books away."

Penelope quickly packed up her things. She was a little surprised at having to take this test, but she was confident in her ability to pass it. And since they all seemed to know enough—other than Xena—they'd be able to start the physical training even sooner.

Which was good because that had to be the most crucial part of joining the military, right?

Herja was the first to be done, and she handed in her paper, then returned to her seat and pulled out a book to read. Penelope found it distracting. She hunched over her page and put her arm up to block it.

Next, Odele finished. Then Nolen. Finally, Penelope had finished answering all her questions and handed in her paper. Xena turned in his paper, which surprisingly had writing on it.

"I will grade these tonight," Professor Farrow said as they stood. "Now. Since we have so much time, I will take you to the obstacle course and let you watch the third-years do their training."

The students all stood, and Penelope shoved her things into her bag. Her brow furrowed as she slung it over her back. Did she really wake up early and rush to get here on time, only for the class to be canceled?

She hoped this wouldn't be a common problem... but judging by the way Herja and Odele were now eyeing each other, Penelope thought there might be a different sort of problem on the horizon.

CHAPTER
SEVEN

Wickham followed Kaia as she skipped through the doorway to their classroom. The morning studies had all been about the history of witches and their role in the Kingdom. Wickham wasn't sure why since this was all stuff he'd learned in basics.

He was excited about this afternoon, though. There were four other witches in their year. The three girls, Jalene, Adina, and Lena—he was going to have trouble keeping all their names apart—and then one other boy, Icarus.

A tall, imposing figure with a bald head, wearing the formal blue uniform, stood in the classroom as Wickham and Kaia entered. Professor Lee's bushy, silver eyebrows came together as he glanced at them.

Wickham knew the other four students were already there and rushed for his spot while Kaia stepped up to Professor Lee.

"We went for a walk in the orchard, and I brought apples for every-one," she said as she lifted the basket in her arms. "Where shall I put them?"

"You can take your seat and pass them out," Professor Lee said.

Wickham let out a heavy breath. Right. This particular professor wanted to be referred to by name only. He seemed to be a friendly, jovial sort of man. It was still tricky for Wickham to think of him without his title... it seemed rude.

He put his backpack on the floor but didn't reach to take anything out of it just yet.

"There is going to be a change in this year's curriculum," Lee said as Kaia passed out the apples. "Normally, we wouldn't go to the Silent Marshes until the spring. The autumn semester is dedicated to the basics of magic and how to use it responsibly. However, due to our current political situation, the Institute has decided that we'll change that."

"What?" Wickham demanded. His hands clenched around an apple. He had to fight the urge to jump to his feet and rush out the door.

Lee focused on him and opened his mouth, but before he could speak, Adina interrupted.

"Political situation? You mean, the change of king and queen?" Her face looked rather pale.

"Yes," Lee replied.

Kaia's face twisted in confusion while Wickham still tried to process this. "I don't understand. Why would that influence our schooling?"

Lee held up his hands as the other students murmured among themselves as well. "Give me some time to answer Kaia's question."

"I already know why," Adina murmured as she buried her face in her hands.

Wickham's heart ached for the girl.

He waited until everyone fell silent before he lowered his hands again. "Normally, it wouldn't change anything for a situation like this. However, you were all part of the attempted kidnapping by Odentia last year. We have decided it will be better to go to the Silent Marshes for your first quest before the change in case Odentia decides to... cause trouble in the weeks leading up to the Coronation."

Wickham's heart thudded in his throat. What did that mean? Were they going to go to war? It seemed impossible, yet... it was also inconceivable that Odentian warriors could sneak into the heart of their Kingdom, yet they did.

"I'm not going," he said, getting to his feet. His hands trembled as he picked his backpack up. "I'm going home."

"Wickham," Kaia explained in surprise. "Why—"

Wickham shook his head, causing his long braid to snap around him. "I'm going home! I didn't want to come to the Institute in the first place. I wanted to stay with my family. And now, instead of being here, we're going to run off to some stupid swamp?"

He knew he shouldn't be talking like this, but he couldn't stop. He had counted on the extra months to prepare mentally to be even further away from his family. To have it sprung on him like this was unthinkable!

"I don't want to be here, either," Adina said as she pushed herself to her feet. "But we're witches; we have to be."

Wickham shook his head again. "I'm going to study from a distance. I'll come back next semester to go the swamp."

"Sit down," Lee said.

His voice was soft, far softer than the near-yelling Wickham was getting to. Wickham hesitated, wanting just to storm out. But something about Lee's gentleness made him sink back into his seat. This wasn't fair. None of this was fair.

"I understand this is hard for you, and I'm sorry that the plans have changed so rapidly," Lee said. His voice remained soft. "All of your parents have been informed of the change, and we have obtained special messenger hawks that will fly continual messages to your families."

Adina buried her face in her arms again.

Wickham slumped back in his chair, ignoring the worried look Kaia was giving him. "Messenger hawks won't give us time to come back if something goes wrong, though."

"We will have medics—"

"I meant with our families!" Tears pricked Wickham's eyes. "Last year, I went to the Silver Springs, and when I got back, my father was sick, and my baby sister was sent away to stop her from getting sick, too. I would have known if I'd been home, even if I couldn't do anything."

Arms wrapped around him. Wickham stiffened until he realized it was Kaia.

"It's going to be okay, you know," she murmured.

"But it might not be."

"It will," Kaia said more firmly. "Your parents will look after things; if anything happens to them, the Crown will look after your siblings. You know that, Wick."

"I suppose," Wickham muttered.

Kaia pulled back and smiled at him. "It's going to be okay. The Silent Marshes will be a great place to visit. You'll see."

"They are beautiful," Lee agreed. "And a very relaxing, peaceful place to be. Not that it's without its dangers. There are nymphs who like to trick people into getting stuck in the bogs. Brownies who will steal your food and left shoes. Only the left shoe, though. And, of course, the Emerald Rattleback."

Wickham sat back in his seat, folding his hands on the desk. "What's that?"

"A giant snake, bigger than a dragon," Lee said.

"I hate snakes," Icarus mumbled.

Lee laughed. "The Rattleback doesn't attack people unless you threaten its nest. Even then, it will leave you alone as soon as you leave its nest alone. Besides, it stays in the heart of the marshes, and we'll stick to the edges. But you need to find the shed skin of the snake for the covers of your spell books."

Adina lifted her head again. She seemed to be crying still but appeared to have brought herself under better control.

"The spell book is the most important tool a witch can have," Lee said.

Adina sniffed. "I've seen one before, but it was blank."

"The only person who can read a witch's spell book is the witch who wrote it. Though there are some commonalities to spells, each one is unique to the witch who uses it is. Unfortunately, we can't share our spells. They don't work for anyone else."

Wickham nodded. He'd learned that much from Kassandra in her herbalist shop.

"If you need to leave this lesson, you may do so now or any time you feel like it's becoming too much," Lee continued gently. "I understand this is a lot, emotionally. We will review basic spells for the next week before heading to the marsh."

Icarus, who until now had been silent, got up and gathered his things. He seemed angry, though Wickham didn't know him well. Adina also left the class. Kaia watched Wickham closely as though she expected him to get up and storm out. The worry in her eyes felt like a mirror. He knew he'd looked that way when watching his sick father at times.

"I think I'm okay now," he told her. "But if it's too much, I'll leave."

Kaia nodded once.

Jalene and Lena were both squirming in their seats, looking distinctly uncomfortable. They kept glancing at one another and then at him.

His outburst had to be uncomfortable for them to witness. Though Wickham's chest tightened with shame for his behavior, he inhaled deeply and faced Professor Lee again. "I want to apologize for how I reacted. I shouldn't have let my anger get the best of me. I'm sorry for being rude."

Lee nodded at him. "Thank you for recognizing that, Wickham."

"I also want to apologize to my fellow students," Wickham continued. He turned to Kaia, Lena, and Jalene. "I'm sorry for having such an outburst and making you uncomfortable. This news affects all of us, and I was acting like I was the only one in the room. I will do my best not to make that mistake again."

"Thanks," Lena muttered.

Jalene just sort of shrugged.

Kaia smiled. "Thanks, Wick. Now. How about we start our lessons?

If we're going to the swamp, I want to know how to keep the bugs away."

Wickham stared at her from the corner of his eye. He marveled she would be so put-together and relaxed about all this. It had to have also taken her by surprise, but she just took it so easily. Was she tamping it down, or did she really just ride the waves as they came at her?

"We won't be going over any spells today, Kaia," Lee said. He seemed more relaxed now, too. "I'd like to talk more about the swamps and what flora and fauna can be found there. There are some extremely rare plants that can't be found anywhere else, and no witch has been successful at propagating them."

Wickham straightened. Rare plants? While he still didn't really want to go, and he was unhappy that these plans had been sprung on him, he tried to push aside his own upset feelings to focus on Lee's teaching.

There might be a way for him to find reasons to be excited to go to the Silent Marshes after all.

TWO WEEKS LATER, they were at the swamp. Kaia's head was about to burst with everything Professor Lee had been teaching them. It would be easy to forget it all, but she had taken plenty of notes and planned to keep her book with her at all times.

"Gather around," Lee called as their dragon escort flew back toward the Institute.

Kaia happily took up a spot in the ring of stumps around an open fireplace. By this time, Wickham seemed much more relaxed about being here, as did Icarus and Adina. In fact, Adina's parents had come to the Institute at one point, and the three of them had a long talk, though Kaia didn't know what it was about, exactly.

The only dragon who stayed behind was Lee's mate, though Kaia hadn't yet learned her name yet.

"We all know that the Silent Marshes are both beautiful and sacred," Lee said as he stood before them. "But they can also be dangerous, remember. Never go into the swamps without a buddy, your compass, and the protective powders I gave you. Understood?"

Kaia raised her hand.

"Yes?" Lee asked her.

"Where's the bathroom?"

A few of the others laughed. Lee pointed to a log building some distance away. "That building has freshly dug pit toilets. There are five toilets, so I don't want to hear any fighting about it."

Kaia frowned. "But what about baths and showers?"

"You'll have to learn to live with the stink or develop a spell to wash it away," Lee replied. "Let's get our camp set up. Curfew will be at dusk each night. When the darkness falls, the protections go up."

The girls had one tent to share, the boys another. Kaia couldn't help but feel sorry for Wickham, only having Icarus for company. She pulled out the girl's tent, eager to finish the work so they could start exploring.

"This is going to be fun," she said to Adina. "I've never gone camping before."

"I haven't either." Adina offered her a small smile.

"We get to learn together!"

Adina's smile widened, and she suddenly hugged her. "Thank you, Kaia. I think I might actually look forward to this now."

"So... you had a good talk with your parents?" Kaia asked hesitantly.

"Yeah. They said the same thing you did. Once I graduate from the Institute, if I haven't found something I want to do, I can go ahead and get further education wherever I want. Even though they dedicated so much of their lives to helping in such a public way, I don't have to."

Kaia grinned. "Good! See, I told you it was going to be okay."

"Yeah." Adina stared at her with a soft light in her eyes. "You really did."

For some reason, the way Adina looked at her made her blush. Kaia quickly got back to work. "Let's get this done. I want to see the orchids."

"All right," Adina said. She sounded... disappointed.

But why? Kaia wasn't sure she wanted to know the answer. She hated to upset people... but maybe she was just reading Adina wrong... she hoped she was.

CHAPTER

EIGHT

P enelope pulled her hair into a bun, ensuring she looked presentable in her loose-fitting tunic and trousers. Satisfied, she glanced at the two empty beds in her room. It just figured that she'd be alone in her room two weeks into her first semester.

She really didn't enjoy being alone like this. Even when she had her own tent with the Fire Watch, she could still hear noises around the camp. These stone walls muffled everything.

She was mainly upset that she had had little time with Wickham and Kaia before they left for the marshes. She wasn't entirely sure that she and Herja could get along without them.

It was raining, so training today would be in the atrium. She was just happy that it was an exercise day... Penelope was finding the studying tedious. Herja always knew the answers to everything, and whenever they had coursework, she paired with Penelope... nobody else wanted to.

Penelope was the last person to arrive at the atrium, arriving just in time for class to start. Professor Farrow nodded in greeting but otherwise didn't comment on her almost-lateness.

"Let's start with some gentle warmups," the Professor said, rolling his shoulders. "We will work on our flexibility today."

Herja leaned over to Penelope as she took her place. "You're late."

"I'm right on time," Penelope replied under her breath.

"If you're not early, you're late," Herja said.

Penelope rolled her eyes. "And if you're late, you die?" she asked sarcastically.

Herja's expression darkened, and she moved to Nolen's other side.

If you just stopped trying to make everyone else as intense as you, you'd have a much easier time, Penelope thought, but then breathed out and released her tension.

Being angry at Herja didn't help her own situation at all.

After warmups, the class entered some stretches. Professor Farrow moved through the group, correcting postures here and there quietly. Soft flute music played somewhere among the thick, leafy atrium, creating a peaceful air.

"Flexibility is essential in our line of work. Raw strength is one thing, but if we don't treat our bodies the right way, they won't be able to do what we need them to do." Professor Farrow stopped near Penelope. "Try to keep your back straight. If you must bend your needs, go ahead."

Penelope tried to feel out her body, to understand what it felt like to have things be in the right place. She bent her knees softly and felt her spine straighten.

"Your knees are too bent," Herja said.

Penelope looked up to see Herja near Xena, pointing at his knees. Irritation was apparent on Xena's face as he moved away from her. "I'm fine; focus on your own posture. How would you like it if I was always correcting you?"

"If you have any tips, I'd be happy to hear them," Herja replied.

Penelope glanced at Professor Farrow. They were frowning, though it appeared they were going to wait to see if Herja and Xena could work this out between them.

"You talk too much; there's a tip," Xena said.

Vera straightened out of her position. "You guys are disturbing everyone. Why are you always trying to boss us around, Herja? Let us figure things out on our own, or let Professor Farrow take care of things."

Professor Farrow cleared their throat. "Please return to your stretches."

It was odd to Penelope that the Professor didn't chastise any students for the disruptions. She wondered why that was. Did Professor Farrow think the students needed to figure these things out themselves? Or was it more about observing them and determining their strengths and weaknesses?

Penelope also found it odd that Herja's expression hardened. She went back into her stretch, pulling it too hard—Penelope could see how the pain flashed over Herja's face—and ignored the surrounding students.

Herja wanted to have friends, didn't she? She was awkward about it and acted like she was too tough and busy to spend time with the others, but she still wanted something from the other students... didn't she?

Trying to figure out Herja was hard. It was as though she had decided nobody should be allowed to be close to her for some reason and did her best to push them away while wishing they'd stay.

Just one more reason Wickham and Kaia would be good to have around. They seem to know how to deal with people.

A thought occurred to Penelope. Maybe, what she needed was some 'backup,' so to say... if Kaia and Wickham weren't here, who else could she go to? The teachers. Herja had been here for over a year, after all. If anyone knew how to get through to her, it would be the people who had been here that whole time as well.

Class was long and strangely challenging for stretching in such a lovely place. Once Professor Farrow dismissed them, Penelope hung back while the others shuffled off.

"Professor, may I talk with you?" Penelope asked.

Professor Farrow nodded, though their expression showed no emotion. "What can I do for you, Penelope?"

"You remember how Herja said she wanted to be Queen one day in the first class?"

"Of course." The Professor smiled as though thinking of something else.

"How can I help her?" No point in beating around the bush. "What I mean is, she doesn't have very good social skills. She's getting on everyone's nerves, and I know she doesn't mean to. If she's going to be Queen one day, she needs to get better at it."

"This is true."

Penelope waited a moment, then sighed. "So, how do I help her, then?"

"With Herja, being blunt is best. Don't hint, and don't sugar coat. Tell her directly, and she will do her best to change that behavior."

"Direct," Penelope said. Her brows pinched together. "But isn't that rude?"

Professor Farrow only smiled. "Rudeness is in the eye of the beholder."

They walked away, and Penelope watched. What was that supposed to mean?

HERJA FROWNED after Penelope as the other girl led her toward the pond. They wouldn't be working in muddy terrain for another week, yet Penelope suggested they try the course around the water.

But Penelope wasn't the sort of person who went against what they were told, so why would she be doing this? Unless she realized that Herja was right about this sort of thing, they needed to get a leg up.

"Should we start with the drag weights?" Herja said once they arrived. Rain sprinkled on their heads, reminding Herja of the day she'd hurt her ankle.

Penelope turned to her. "No. I asked you to come here so we could talk privately."

Herja backed up a step. No. She knew it. Penelope didn't like her.

She was going to tell Herja to leave her alone and stop pairing with her during class.

"I'm not entirely sure how to say this," Penelope continued. "I talked to Professor Farrow, and they suggested I should just be blunt about it."

"You had to ask the Professor?" Herja clenched her fists. "You can't just tell me you don't like me and not to bother you anymore?"

Penelope's eyebrows, growing into a deeper, wine-red shade, drew into a V. "What? No, that's not what I'm trying to say at all."

Herja stared at her uncertainly. "It's not?"

"No."

"But... but I annoy everyone. Why aren't you annoyed?"

Penelope shook her head and rolled her eyes. "Of course I'm annoyed! You're very annoying with how you act like you know everything more than everyone else. But I know that you're not just like that. I read all your letters, remember?"

Herja opened her mouth and shut it again. Thunder boomed in the air, and she screamed, throwing herself to the ground.

"Herja?"

No, no. Go away! "Rain, rain, go away, come again another day," she sang. The other children at the orphanage used to sing it. Maybe if she was loud enough—

Penelope knelt beside her. "Herja?"

"I can't... thunder... we gotta get inside!" Herja leaped to her feet. She seized Penelope's hand and raced back toward the building, dragging Penelope with her.

Lightning.

Thunder.

Some part of her knew that she'd move faster if she weren't pulling Penelope. But the idea of leaving her friend out here to face the storm herself was even more abhorrent. Herja continued, trying to sing loud enough to drown out the storm.

When they got into the Institute, Herja slammed the door behind them. Her legs were weak, and she oozed to the floor like all her bones had disappeared. Then, she buried her face into her arms and started to sob.

At some point, Penelope suggested they return to the dorm to get into dry clothes and warm up. Herja hid her face, not wanting anyone else to know that she had been crying.

Penelope led her into her own room and offered Herja fleece pajamas to change into. Herja was too tired to protest, so she did. And when Penelope suggested she lie down for a bit before supper, she did that, too. Penelope looked awkward as she sat at her desk chair and rearranged her books.

By this time, despite her lingering fear whenever light flashed outside, Herja felt somewhat... silly.

"What did you want to talk to me about, anyway?" she asked, turning to her side to look at Penelope.

"It doesn't matter; it can wait."

"But if it will help me not to annoy people... I'd like to know." Herja burrowed herself deeper into the blankets.

Penelope shifted around her books for a moment longer before she shrugged. "Well... the way you talk to us, always correcting us like we should know what you're talking about already, is frustrating. It makes us feel like you think we're stupid."

"I don't mean to make you feel that way."

"I know. Which is why I can put up with you." Penelope winked at her. "But the others don't know that. So, I think if you just work on that. Listening to other people and not thinking that you need to prove how smart you are always."

Herja nodded once. "Thank you. I'll work on that."

She turned over and closed her eyes as she thought about Penelope's words, the behavior of other students and others in the orphanage before that was clearer. No wonder they called her things like smarty-pants. She hadn't realized they were making fun of her before now.

Herja sighed. She still had a lot to learn.

CHAPTER
NINE

T he smell was horrendous.

As peaceful and beautiful as the Silent Marshes may be, Kaia didn't want to spend months here. After a few days, she thought she was used to the scent. Today was particularly bad, however. She pinched her nose shut with one hand as she picked her way over fallen branches.

"I always thought that the Silent Marshes would be more soupy," her buddy for the day said.

Kaia glanced over her shoulder. Adina had spent much more time with her and Wickham since they started camping. She was still sure that Adina looked at her the same way some boys at the palace did, but it hadn't affected their friendship so far.

There wasn't any reason it should, really.

"The ground is pretty firm," Kaia said. Her voice sounded muffled and nasally. "Maybe more of the marsh is deeper into the forest, and that's why it smells so bad today because the wind is pushing it toward us?"

"That's probably it," Adina agreed.

They had been searching for almost five hours now, searching for some sign of shed snakeskin. No luck.

"Kaia, can I ask you something?" Adina asked, sounding a little stiff.

"Sure."

"What do you hope your fated mate will be like?"

Kaia pondered the question. She stopped to lean against a tree for rest. "Well, he has to have a good sense of humor. A kind smile. It'd be great if he read a lot, but I suppose that's unnecessary."

Adina's face fell. "He? What if your fated mate is a girl?"

"I don't think so. But when you think about it, there are four girls and two boys among us witches, and our fated mates will be the first-year dragons. There are also two boys and four girls among the dragons. Which means..." Kaia frowned as she figured it out in her head. "There are twelve of us, which means we're going to have at least two pairs of fated mates be two girls together."

"But you don't think you'll be one of them?" Adina pressed.

Kaia considered for a long moment what to say. "Witches aren't paired with witches, Adina."

Adina's cheeks turned red. "I know that."

"I'm not attracted to girls," Kaia continued, trying to keep her voice gentle. "At least, not yet. I haven't really been attracted to boys yet, either. Maybe I won't be attracted to either; I don't know. What I can say is that I don't want to have any sort of attractions right now."

"Oh." Adina fidgeted. "Why?"

"I had cousins who developed feelings and relationships when they were fourteen, only to have their hearts broken when the ceremony took place." Kaia wrapped her arms around herself. "Mama and Papa say that fourteen is far too young to start with all that messiness, and I agree."

"My mother and father started to date when they were fourteen," Adina argued. "And I think they are very happy together. They were fated mates, too."

Kaia shook her head. "My mama would say that's the exception, not the rule."

She'd had long internal discussions about these sorts of things but never talked about it out loud. Truth be told, the idea of having someone in your life that you were matched with forever terrified her. She was glad she had until the end of the next school year before she had to deal with it.

"Look," Kaia said, moving a little closer. "I think you're a great friend. I would like us to remain friends. But that's all we can be, okay? Friends."

Adina nodded. She looked embarrassed, and Kaia couldn't look at her for too long.

"I—" Kaia continued, wanting to reassure Adina, to let her know her feelings were okay or something.... She wasn't sure how she was meant to handle this sort of situation.

But at that moment, a loud, cracking noise filled the swamp

"What was that?" Adina cried, jumping closer to Kaia.

"I think it came from this direction," Kaia said, pointing. She hurried along, calling out to see if anyone was in trouble.

A glowing light caught her eye just ahead. She slowed slightly as a warm, fuzzy feeling washed over her. It was like someone had wrapped a warm blanket around her brain. The tension she'd held as she talked to Adina disappeared.

What a beautiful light.

Kaia wanted to see it closer. A voice sang softly as she made her way toward the light. She was aware of other movement around her, but she didn't look to see what was causing them... she just wanted to get closer to that beautiful light.

Suddenly, the light was blocked out. Adina's face loomed in Kaia's vision, and Adina's hands clapped over her ears. Kaia cried out, furious...

And then, the anger was gone.

Kaia blinked rapidly, her head spinning like she'd been running in circles for hours. Her stomach churned.

"What?" she asked, then had to stop because she felt like she was about to vomit.

Adina snatched the protective powders off Kaia's belt, pushed one vial into Kaia's hand, and then covered her ears again.

Of course! Kaia quickly took out a pinch of the blue powder and put it on the tip of her tongue—the protective spell wrapped around her, easing her nausea. Kaia stepped back and glanced over Adina's shoulder. The light was still there, but no longer had that same draw. In the center of the light was a tiny, laughing figure.

All four of their classmates were walking toward it, their steps stumbling, their eyes blank.

"Quick," Adina said, her voice calm despite the situation. "We need to get them to take the protective spells."

WICKHAM WAS WALKING among the clouds. Everything was warm, joyful, and bright. The little creature beckoned him forward, promising a world of no more worries. He could bring his family with him... there was candy there that didn't rot your teeth. Tara and the twins could eat as much as they wanted—

A set of hands covered his ears. Another set covered his mouth. Something was put in his mouth, and he gagged on the bitter taste.

The surrounding warmth faded away. When the hands were removed from his eyes, he was no longer among the clouds but in a boggy spot of marsh with water seeping through his shoes.

Kaia and Adina both stepped back from him. They looked him up and down, then nodded in satisfaction.

"That's everyone," Adina said.

"We did a good job," Kaia replied. She grinned and high-fived Adina.

Wickham sat on a half-rotten long and groaned. "What was that?"

"A nymph," Kaia replied, crouching near him. "Are you okay?"

"I... will be?" Wickham replied. He'd never had a headache like this before. It was clearing rapidly, though; if he could lie down for a couple of minutes, he'd be okay.

A whimpering noise caught his attention. Jalene crouched on the ground next to Lena. Both of Lena's hands were wrapped around her knee; there was a smear of blood on her pant leg.

Instantly, Wickham jumped to his feet. He ignored his own nausea as he headed over, reaching into his herb pouch.

"It's not deep," he said as he pulled a lavender resin out. "Here, chew on this."

Lavender didn't help with pain; he'd have to make a tea. Best to give Lena something to do, something that she could think was helping, as he took care of her injury. He used water from his waterskin to clean the wound out, then clean bandages to wrap it.

"Can you walk?" Wickham asked once he was done.

Lena put on a brave face as she slowly got to her feet. She stumbled, then cried out. Wickham had to catch her and brace her.

"Carry me," she whimpered.

"I don't think I can," Wickham replied, his brow furrowing. "But if we all try together—"

"Never mind, I think I can walk after all," Lena said quickly.

She walked forward without so much as a limp. Wickham scratched his head but ensured everyone was together as they headed back to camp.

Once there, Adina explained what had happened to their professor. Lee listened with an intent expression, then nodded. "You did a good job thinking quickly like that. We'll have to be more careful if there's a nymph in the area that could catch all of you at once."

Wickham cleared his throat. "Lena was hurt. I did the best I could, but it probably needs a proper cleaning, and she needs some painkillers."

"Thank you, Wickham. In that case, please get some water boiling and mix a kettle for willow tea while I get the protections up for the night."

Wickham nodded once and set to work. Kaia immediately got the food out for supper while Icarus went to his tent, and Jalene sat with Lena, talking to her in a low voice. Adina stoked up the fire.

Once everything was ready, Lee had the students gather around.

"Wickham, since you already know so much about treating minor injuries, you can help me."

Wickham crouched near the teacher, eager to assist.

"Being able to heal small wounds is an important part of any witch's repertoire," Lee said as he unwound the bandage around Lena's leg. "But an important thing to remember is that it takes energy and the body's resources to heal injuries. It's always best, then, to work with the body and make slight movements so as not to overly exhaust your patient."

Wickham nodded along. He knew this; Kassandra had told him.

"So, we want to work with the herbs and plants that the earth has given us to help the body do its best work," Lee continued. "Wick, can you explain to the class how to make willow bark tea and why it's effective?"

Wickham jumped slightly, not expecting to have the class turned over to him. He cleared his throat, nervous about forgetting something. "There are three steps. The first one is to locate the proper type of willow. White willow is the best. The second would be to peel the bark, then dry and store it."

It occurred to him that they could just find a herbalist to get the willow bark from if they were in normal circumstances. Wickham cleared his throat again, lowering his head, so he didn't have to look at his classmates staring back at him.

"After that, you want to take just a little bit, equivalent to one or two tea bags, and boil them for up to ten minutes. Then there's your tea. You can flavor it if you want. It's easier for the patient to drink it that way."

"And how does it work?" Lee pressed.

"It's got a special compound. I don't remember what it's called. An acid of some sort?"

"That's right."

As Lee explained in more depth, Wickham felt a warmth spread through his chest. He had been useful here... and was learning more than he could at home. He hung on the teacher's every word. When he got home, he'd share it all with Kassandra.

He knew she'd love to hear all the recent findings they taught at school.

CHAPTER
TEN

erja dragged herself into the chair next to Penelope, rubbing the back of her neck. The other first-year dragons were already there with food on the table. Herja served herself. She'd put in an extra hour at the gym after everyone else had finished.

"It was a good training session today, wasn't it?" Herja said, trying to make her voice cheerful like Kaia's would be. "Odele, you're so quick, and you've got excellent control of your kicks."

Since her conversation with Penelope, Herja was trying to be more aware of not criticizing others while noting their good points. She wasn't sure it was making them like her, but it seemed their classmates didn't dislike her any more, at least.

Headmaster Twila stepped up to the podium, and Herja frowned. They shouldn't have any announcements to hear.

"May I have your attention?" the headmaster asked, her voice calling out clearly.

Everyone fell silent.

It appeared Headmaster Twila was briefly lost for words, then she cleared her throat and straightened. "I have sad news. King Diesel passed away last night. We can draw comfort because his passing was peaceful."

Herja's hands grew cold. King Diesel, dead? She had thought he was an older man when she saw him last year, but... but he was the only human king she'd known.

"With King Diesel's passing, Queen Charlize will retire because of her age and health. Our newly-elected human king and queen have been prepared for this leadership change; their Coronation will take place sooner than expected."

Herja didn't want to listen to this anymore. Her hands clenched in her lap as she rubbed them together, trying to warm them up. Even though she'd been starving moments earlier, she didn't want to eat now.

"It's ridiculous; I didn't even know them," she said, and to her frustration, her voice wobbled.

"What did you say?" Odele asked.

But rather than being scandalized, she sounded sad as well. Herja inhaled and lifted her head. Moisture pooled in her eyes, and she rubbed it away. "Just talking to myself. I hope Kaia is doing all right. She knew King Diesel. She spent the summer at the palace...."

Penelope pushed herself from the table. "Look, Headmaster Twila is leaving; let's talk to her and see if we can go out to the Silent Marshes to see Kaia."

Herja was more than happy for the excuse to leave the table. She chased Penelope without even confirming that what she said was true.

It made little sense that her chest felt like an elephant was sitting on it. It made little sense that she was fighting these tears... but all Herja could think about was how sad this would make Kaia. The last thing she wanted was her bright, bubbly friend to be sad.

Not that Herja could do anything about it. She couldn't bring the dead back to life, after all.

"Where did the headmaster go?" Herja asked once they were out of the dining hall.

"I think this way?" Penelope led her down the hallway that led to the offices.

Given how old Headmaster Twila was, it seemed impossible for them to have lost track of her already. There was no sound of her footsteps, though, and when they rounded the corner, there was no sign of the headmaster.

Herja frowned. "Maybe she went to her office?"

"That's a good idea." Penelope gestured toward the corridor.

They headed toward the headmaster's office on the third floor, next to the atrium.

Should she ask Penelope how she was doing? Or was this quest of theirs the only thing keeping Penelope from breaking down, too?

They reached the office to find the door slightly ajar. Voices came from inside, and Herja let out a relieved breath. Soon this would be over, and she wouldn't have to feel anymore. They could go to the Silent Marshes, and she could focus on managing Kaia's feelings rather than facing her own.

As they approached, Headmaster Valiant's voice met Herja's ears. And the words he said stopped her dead.

"There's no reason to tell the students that we might be on the brink of war."

Penelope grabbed Herja's arm, her eyes wide.

"We don't know anything for certain," Headmaster Valiant continued. "Just the rumor that he ordered his armies to march on the western borders. Even Odentia's king can't be so arrogant as to think he can face down an army of dragons and witches."

"And if we are to go to war? These students could graduate to the battle zone." Twila's tone was hardened with stress. "We might have dragons and witches, but their armies are bigger than ours. Even with human volunteers to swell our ranks, many lives would be lost on both sides."

Herja had never heard adults that stressed before.

"Let's hope it doesn't come to that," Valiant replied grimly.

THE BRINK OF WAR? Penelope's whole body seemed to be flooded with ice. She could hardly breathe as her fingers dug into Herja's arm. If her grip hurt the other girl, Herja showed no signs of it. Her eyes were wide, her expression mirroring the horror that Penelope felt.

We shouldn't be here. This isn't for our ears, Penelope thought.

She turned to run but stopped as a figure in a blue uniform approached. Her heart jumped to her throat, and her mouth dropped open, ready to make up some excuse for herself.

But Professor Farrow's ordinarily stoic expression was soft. They gestured for the two girls to follow them, then knocked on the door of the headmaster's office.

"You have a couple of eavesdroppers," the professor said, ushering the two in.

Headmaster Valiant rubbed his temples. "How much did you hear?"

"Too much," Penelope said.

Herja stepped forward, her back ramrod straight, and her chin lifted. "Are we really going to war?"

The headmasters glanced at each other. Penelope desperately hoped they would say, of course not, that they were just joking around... but she knew in her heart that if they did say such a thing, she could never trust them again.

As much as she didn't want the truth, she knew she needed it.

"There is some sign that Odentia will become aggressive," Headmaster Twila spoke. "Queen Abigail and King Sydney's youngest daughter, Adina, is with the first-year witches at the Silent Marshes. We believe Odentia may try to abduct her while she is vulnerable."

Penelope found that the air seemed to be getting thinner. She sucked in greedy breaths, trying not to panic. "But why would they do that?"

"Odentia wants magic," Headmaster Valiant replied. "They seem to think that if we gave them water from the Silver Springs, they would have all the wealth they want."

Penelope couldn't understand it. She had taken part in relief efforts when Odentia suffered major flooding. She and Momma had both gone to their kingdom to help; if they needed more supplies, why wouldn't they just ask?

"So, they want to steal the magic?" Herja said, her brow furrowed. "And they think that by kidnapping Adina, they'll be able to force the new king and queen into giving it to them?"

"It's possible, yes," Headmaster Twila admitted. "Which is why we will bring the first-year witches back to the Institute at once."

Yes. Immediate action. That was good. Penelope's mind raced. She could help with that. Even though she wasn't a fighter and wasn't anywhere near ready to defend the Kingdom, she could help with evacuations. Through her years with the Fire Watch, she had participated in plenty of evacuations. She knew what to do.

"I would like to volunteer to go with the team to the Silent Marshes and help to bring them back," she said, straightening herself up.

Headmaster Twila gazed at her with some sort of emotion that Penelope couldn't decipher. "That's very brave of you. I know that you both want to help your friends. The best thing you can do right now, though, is to focus on your studies."

"But—" Herja started.

"Herja. Penelope." Headmaster Twila's voice grew firm. "Believe me; I understand how you feel. If you were trained, I wouldn't hesitate to accept your help. The fact is, however, that neither of you has the training for this sort of mission. Speed is of the essence, and unfortunately, you will slow the retrieval."

Penelope's shoulders slumped. "But I have so much experience with evacuations."

Headmaster Twila nodded. "You do. And if it were an evacuation, you would have the experience to help. This isn't, however. We are sending our six fastest dragons alone, with only enough supplies to keep them going, to bring the first-year witches back to the Institute. So, you see, there isn't room for you."

"Oh." Penelope ran a hand through her hair. "You have it in hand, then."

"We do," Headmaster Valiant confirmed.

Herja cleared her throat. "Do you want us to keep this to ourselves? Not alarm the other students?"

"That would be preferable, yes, but you won't be punished if you speak of it," Headmaster Valiant said. "Farrow?"

"Yes, Headmaster?"

"Will you escort our young dragons back to the dining hall?" Headmaster Twila asked.

Herja snorted. "Do you think we can eat now?"

"You should try. You need your strength," the headmaster said simply.

Penelope looped her arm around Herja's. "Understood. We will do our best."

As she and Herja turned out of the room, Penelope's mind raced. She needed to get to the Silent Marshes... but how?

CHAPTER
ELEVEN

Wickham's eyes burned with the need for sleep, but he fought it as he searched the densely packed foliage for a splash of yellow among all the shades of green.

"I haven't had a proper sleep since we got here," he complained as he scrambled over a low log. "I don't see how Lee thinks we'll be able to find anything when we're so exhausted all the time."

Kaia, his buddy on this trip into the swamp, made a non-committal noise in her throat. "I've been sleeping just fine. What's been keeping you up at night? Maybe you should ask the professor for a sleeping aid."

She brushed her hand through some low grass, revealing the yellow flowers they were looking for... but she just sighed and moved on with a distracted look.

"Hey, they're right here!" Wickham pointed. He tugged on Kaia's sleeve while gesturing to what she had just uncovered.

Kaia blinked. Then her shoulders slumped, and her cheeks darkened. "Oh. I... I guess I wasn't paying attention."

Wickham knelt beside the flowers. He carefully plucked them off and placed them into the pouch at his waist. "You seem very distracted for someone who is sleeping just fine," he mentioned.

"I... haven't been sleeping well," Kaia admitted. Her brow furrowed.

"You just said you were sleeping fine."

"Did I?"

Wickham straightened, frowning at her. "What's wrong? You're not usually this scatterbrained."

Kaia bit her lip, rocking on her toes as she looked away. "It's... well. I had to turn someone down who was interested in me. Romantically. I didn't expect something like that to happen here, and I keep wondering if I was too harsh... then I wonder if I was too gentle, and I'm leading her on."

"Her?" Wickham repeated. "So not Icarus?"

"I don't think it's right for me to tell you who she is," Kaia said. She shrugged as she knelt and helped pick the flowers. "I just don't... I don't understand romantic attraction. Not yet, at least. It just seems all so weird... I'd rather wait until I know who my fated mate is and then learn to fall in love with them."

"I don't think you learn how to fall in love," Wickham said. "I think it just happens."

Kaia tilted her head, her silver curls brushing against her shoulder. "Do you have any interests, then? Romantically, I mean?"

Wickham felt heat rising in his cheeks. "Not at the time being, no. I've had crushes before, but they've never lasted long. I know the sort of girl I want for my fated mate. Though, I know it's not up to me in the end. I try not to think about it too much."

He didn't want to explain more about how he had dreamt of finding the perfect partner for himself, who fit into his family... right until it was revealed he was a witch. Then, knowing that his fated mate would be assigned to him, Wickham had pushed aside all those feelings and did his best not to think about it anymore. Humans had it so much easier, they could choose for themselves.

The dragon-witch bond was one of the strongest bonds there was in life, or so he had been told. Wickham knew that fated mates always ended up together romantically, even if they fought it at first. That didn't mean he liked the idea of someone being chosen for him.

But he also knew that it was different for Kaia. She had expected to be a dragon or a witch from the time she was little. So, she had always believed that she would have a fated mate one day.

"I'm glad you're the same way about relationships, I mean," Kaia said as she handed him the flowers she'd picked. "I've been getting a lot of attention over the past year... everyone has been very respectful toward me, but I still don't like that type of attention. I don't feel ready."

Wickham opened his mouth, then closed it again. He wasn't sure how to respond to that. He could only hope that he'd made no one uncomfortable in his past when he had a crush on them... of course, he had always done his best to hide it, being embarrassed to like someone so deeply.

Finally, he cleared his throat. "What about it makes you uncomfortable?"

Kaia shrugged.

"You must have some idea."

"I don't really, though. Oh... I guess that's not entirely true," Kaia admitted. She toyed with the hem of her frilly shirt for a moment. "I don't like the idea of hurting someone's feelings because of something they can't help."

"You can't help it, either."

Kaia sighed. "I guess."

Wickham took her hand in his, squeezing comfortingly the way his mother would do for him. "Is this something you need to talk to Lee about? If this person is bothering you...."

Kaia shook her head. "They're not. She and I have resolved the situation already. I'm just having a hard time with it, is all."

"If you need to talk about it more, I'm here," Wickham offered. He didn't enjoy seeing her upset.

Kaia gave him a distracted smile. "Thanks. It's getting a little late. We should head back to camp."

Wickham nodded, putting their discussion from his mind. He didn't want to dwell on whatever romances he would have in the future. It would happen, or maybe it wouldn't—the important thing was that he would concentrate on his schooling and prepare for his future career, not waste energy worrying about romance.

They hadn't gone far before the hair on the back of Wickham's neck stood on end. He grabbed Kaia's arm, stopping her as he looked around. It was the same feeling he'd gotten one summer when he went early to work in the fields. It had been the most unnerving feeling... later he learned a mountain lion was in the area.

"What is it?" Kaia asked.

Her voice seemed startlingly loud in the swamp's stillness. Wickham hushed her, straining his eyes and ears.

There! They heard a low-thumping noise that seemed out of place. Putting his fingers to his lips to show to Kaia that they needed to stay quiet, Wickham crept forward.

His heart jumped into his throat as they approached the bushes' edge. Half a dozen warriors in Odentian armor were standing over Adina and Icarus. Both of them were unconscious. Wickham's hands clenched into fists as one warrior, wearing a plumed helmet, grabbed Adina's limp form and slung her over his back.

"What about this one, sir?" another warrior asked.

Whatever he was going to say was cut short as Kaia suddenly leaped from the bushes. Wickham bit back a curse as he followed her, looking for something to defend himself with—all they had were the protective powders.

Kaia opened her mouth.

Wickham had just enough time to think she was about to demand that the Odentian warriors release their classmates when Kaia screamed. The warriors shouted in surprise, but Wickham barely heard them. Kaia's scream was so loud and shrill that it rang through the swamp, echoing back to them.

"Shut up, you brat!" the man with the plumed helmet came at them, swinging his fists.

Moments later, a roar echoed out—the sound of a dragon. The Odentian warriors flinched. Their plumed leader made a hand motion, and they disappeared into the trees. Kaia started to follow, but Wickham grabbed her again.

Their enemies were leaving—meaning they needed to care for their friends.

"Help me with Adina and Icarus," Wickham called.

SOUNDS OF SHOUTING, metal clashing, and screams seemed to follow Kaia and Wickham as they tended to Adina and Icarus. Or rather, as Wickham tended to them. Kaia stood guard, protective powder clenched in both fists as she watched the forest for any sign that the Odentian warriors were returning.

A loud, painful roar.

And everything went silent.

Kaia's hands fell out of their fists, her heart pounding. Her throat was impossibly dry as she backed up, searching for Wickham without taking her eyes off the forest.

What happened? She didn't dare speak, as though the Odentian warriors would return if she did.

Rustling in the bushes behind them made her spin. Kaia screamed as a figure loomed, but her voice cut out when Lee came into the clearing. He had blood on his shirt, and his mate, Claire, followed behind him, one arm tucked around her middle.

"Are you injured?" Wickham asked, jumping to his feet.

"I'm fine," Claire said, though her arm tightened.

"What happened?" Kaia demanded.

Lee ignored her question as he knelt beside the two unconscious teens. "Wick, are they injured?"'

"Not that I can see," Wickham replied. "Unconscious. But I suspect magic was used... although how Odentia got magic, I don't know."

Claire growled. Smoke still trailed from her mouth, and her skin glistened with scales. "No doubt they stole it. Let's get back to camp."

Kaia nodded, relief washing over her. The adults were here; they were taking over. Everything was going to be fine now.

LEE CARRIED ICARUS, while Claire carried Adina. But as they moved their way through the swamp, Wickham could see the dragon's breathing grow more and more shallow.

"We should look at that cut," he finally said.

Claire shook her head. "All I need is a good night's rest."

But rest would not be possible. When they came to camp, they found it completely ransacked. Their supplies smoldered in a pile. The tents were slashed into ribbons. And all the coops for the messenger hawks were open, with the birds missing.

The rest of the students had gathered. Everyone grouped around Lee and Claire, expressions ranging from horrified to shocked and confused.

"The birds," Lena gasped, gesturing to the empty cages. "Did they kill the birds?"

"No, those birds are so friendly; all the Odentian warriors would have to do was give them a pet, and then they could take them anywhere. There's no sign of corpses, is there?" Lee asked. His forehead was wrinkled. "We need to get word to the Institute."

By this time, Adina and Icarus were awake again, though groggy. Adina kept dry heaving, no matter how many herbs Wickham gave her to ease her stomach. Icarus' face was green, but he seemed to handle it better.

"Claire," Lee said, turning to his mate. "Will you be able to carry anyone with you?"

Wickham looked up, his heart thudding. Dragons were big, but not so big that they could carry the entire class... Lee had to have a singular person in mind.

Adina. Because her parents are going to be the new king and queen once King Diesel and Queen Charlize step down. Wickham's shoulders hunched forward. Did that mean that the rest of them were inconsequential? *No, just that Adina is the most vulnerable.*

If that even was what Lee was thinking.

Claire moved her arm to check her wound. Wickham gasped when he saw the amount of blood staining her shirt.

"Sit down right now!" he shouted at her, immediately pulling his herb pouch out again. "A yarrow poultice... yarrow will help staunch the blood. I—"

Lee put his hand over Wickham's. "Wick. Calm down. Dragons heal at an accelerated rate compared to witches and humans."

"I'm not bleeding anymore," Claire added. She lowered her arm and lifted her shirt. She wiped up her stomach, revealing a long, thin line of scar tissue. "Internally is another matter, though... I don't think I can carry anyone without risking opening the wound up again."

Lee nodded once. "Then you fly back to the Institute and warn them about what's happening. I'll take the students deeper into the Silent Marshes. We can use the swamp as protection; we'll work our way to the other side, to the Watch stationed there."

Claire nodded. She kissed Lee, making Wickham look away. "Be safe," she whispered.

She shifted into her dragon form, a huge glittering beast with rainbow scales. Her wings stretched out to either side of her, and Wickham winced, seeing the gashes in the membrane. But Claire took to the air and headed into the dusk.

"Gather whatever you can find," Lee called as he straightened. "We leave in five minutes."

CHAPTER

TWELVE

"*Five green and speckled frogs,*" Herja sang as she dangled over the ground. The sky was clear, with no clouds, no lightning, and yet her heart pounded just as hard as the day she injured herself. She couldn't seem to get herself to let go of this bar so she could grab the next one. "*Sat on a speckled log.*"

Her hands were slick with sweat. She just needed to keep moving... if she could do that, then—

Her fingers slipped off entirely. Herja gasped as she plummeted toward the ground. She bounced in the large net set up beneath the course; the breath knocked from her from the fall but no further damage.

She grabbed one rope, panting as she closed her eyes. Another fall. Another failure.

"Hey!" Penelope called.

Herja twisted over, seeing the other girl heading toward her. With a sigh, Herja pulled herself over the rope net and rolled onto the ground. Penelope's fire-red hair was pulled into a braid, and she wore dark workout clothing.

"You here for—" Herja started.

"Professor Lee's mate has returned from the Silent Marshes," Penelope panted to catch her breath. Her hands were clenched into fists. "The six dragons sent to retrieve the students never arrived. They were ambushed by Odentian warriors."

Herja's heart thudded all the harder. "Kaia and Wickham?"

"I don't know. That's all I heard before I was chased off."

Herja considered it for a moment, trying to calm her racing thoughts. The adults would never just tell them anything... or would they? "Let's go to the headmaster's office. Maybe we can hear something."

Penelope nodded. Together, the two girls took off toward the Institute.

They have to tell us something, Herja thought as they wound through the now-familiar stone hallways. *They can't just keep us in the dark. That wouldn't be fair!*

Not that adults were always fair... just one thing Herja intended to change when she became Queen!

Voices emerged from Headmaster Twila's office, muffled by the thick, heavy door. Penelope got there first and hesitated. Penelope lifted her hand, then pressed her ear to the door instead.

"I can't hear anything. Do you think we should knock?" Penelope asked, turning her gaze to Herja.

Herja had the answer already—but knowing that Penelope wouldn't like it, she simply turned down the handle and strode in. The door opened soundlessly, and the adults were so caught up in their discussion that, at first, they didn't notice the two girls.

"—Need to take stronger measures," Headmaster Twila was saying. "We don't know if the dragons we sent made it or were waylaid."

"Twila," Headmaster Valiant said suddenly.

He put a light, but firm hand on her shoulder and motioned for them to join them. Herja, knowing she'd been caught, walked in further with her shoulders straightened.

"Penelope and I—" she started.

"Herja," Headmaster Valiant interrupted. A dreadfully serious frown replaced his normal easy-going smile. "This is a private discussion. Whatever you and Penelope wish to talk to us about—"

"I'm sorry, but it's about this," Herja stated firmly. She stood straighter. It might be rude to interrupt, but Headmaster Valiant did it first. She threw back her shoulders, ready to argue herself blue in the face if that's what it took. "Penelope heard that Professor Lee's mate returned, saying that the first-year witches had been attacked."

The other professors were all in the room, Herja suddenly realized, along with several other people she didn't know but recognized from around the Institute. Herja felt herself shrinking back under the weight of their stares, but she steeled herself.

Penelope stood beside her silently. Herja wished she would say something.

Herja cleared her throat when nobody, not even any of the adults, said anything. "We have a right to know. Odentia attempted to abduct us last year. You might think this isn't for children to worry about, but we're not little kids anymore. We're both fourteen and only five years from starting our careers."

"Five years is a long time," Headmaster Twila remarked. "I know it doesn't feel like it. I remember what it was like to be fourteen—"

"Were you kidnapped when you were thirteen?" Herja demanded.

Penelope stirred. "Herja is right, Headmasters. We have already been through quite an ordeal. Those are our friends at the Silent Marshes. Odentia has clearly infiltrated the Kingdom again. I know we can't do anything about that. But we can at least know what measures are being taken to retrieve the first-year witches, can't we?"

There was a calmness to Penelope's tone and posture that Herja envied. Penelope seemed so collected. Her stance was as though she expected answers because it was simply logical.

The two headmasters glanced at each other. The professors frowned, and the strangers openly scowled at the two girls. Herja tried her best to ignore them. Some silent conversation passed between the headmasters, and Headmaster Valiant slowly nodded once.

"We are preparing a convoy to the Silent Marshes," Headmaster Twila said.

"Convoy?" Penelope asked.

"With armed forces," Headmaster Valiant confirmed. "To better protect the students once they are found."

Penelope's eyebrows furrowed together, but Herja leaned forward, putting her hands on the headmaster's desk. "That means more than just dragons are going, doesn't it?"

"Headmaster," one of the stranger witches protested. "These children don't need the burden of knowing—"

"So, you're just going to force the burden of not knowing on us?" Herja snapped.

The witch's mouth thinned. "You are very rude. Have you never heard of letting others finish what they're saying?"

"And you are rude for talking about Penelope and me as though we're not in the room," Herja replied.

"Enough," Headmaster Valiant said. Though his voice didn't raise in volume, there was a sharpness to it Herja rarely heard. "We have enough issues to deal with. We don't need to start useless arguments. Herja, please apologize to General Rufus."

Herja scowled but faced the general. "I apologize for interrupting."

General Rufus scoffed and nodded.

"And General?" Valiant said, raising an eyebrow.

The witch stared at him for a moment before his cheeks turned red. He cleared his throat, then said, "I apologize to both of you girls for speaking as though you weren't in the room."

"Thank you, General," Herja replied. She tried to keep her tone and expression smooth. She had found that adults didn't like to apologize to children, and she didn't want to make the general think less of her.

"To answer your question," Headmaster Valiant continued, "yes. The convoy will have human warriors and witches. We want them to be well prepared for any issues they may face."

Penelope hummed. "And you'll have to take supplies with you, too, won't you?"

"Yes," Headmaster Valiant replied.

Herja opened her mouth again, but Penelope took hold of her arm. "You will tell us as soon as there are any developments, right?"

"Of course."

Penelope nodded, then gave a little bow. "Then we apologize for interrupting. We'll leave so you can finalize the details and get our friends back sooner."

"Hey," Herja protested, but Penelope dragged her from the room.

"Shh," Penelope hissed at her.

Herja rolled her eyes but allowed Penelope to guide her away. As they headed toward the dorm rooms, Penelope's head was down as though she was deep in thought.

As soon as they were in the common room, Penelope released Herja's hand.

"What's going on?" Herja demanded.

"Get a pack together. An extra set of clothes and blankets and some light stones. We're going to the Silent Marshes."

THE KITCHEN WAS NEVER ENTIRELY empty except late at night. Penelope convinced the cooks that she needed extra snacks for nighttime because she was waking up hungry every night. Cookies might not be the best form of nutrition, but she got a good lot of them, along with jerky, some bread, and a good-sized bag of nuts.

The pickings might be slim while they snuck off campus, but at least they wouldn't starve.

By the time Penelope had scrounged up six water skins and filled them, Herja was likewise ready to go. Her pack was relatively flat, but when Penelope frowned at it, Herja only smiled.

"Remember my book bag? It's in here, along with anything we need to be comfortable."

Penelope let out a sigh of relief. She had forgotten about that bag. "You said you had one witch shrink it back down."

"It's still big enough for us to fit inside," Herja replied. "I like to hide inside when I don't want to be disturbed. It'll also make it easier for us to stow away... which is what I assume we're doing?"

Penelope nodded. "The adults will never let us go, and I won't sit around her any longer."

Herja smirked at her. "You're the last person I thought would break the rules like this."

"We're not breaking...." Penelope trailed off. They were breaking all sorts of rules by doing this. She didn't have to be told not to sneak into a convoy like this to know she shouldn't be doing it. Her spine stiffened as she lifted her chin. "Maybe we are... but we must hurry if we're going to get there."

They hurried through the corridors and then outside. The convoy was preparing in the middle of the sparring field, gathering supplies into large baskets that the dragons would carry between them. Penelope watched, trying to figure out the best way to sneak in.

"If you get in the bag, I'll get us into the convoy," Herja said. She pulled the book bag, covered in leaves and vines, from her pack.

Penelope glanced at it warily; she didn't relish the idea of being jostled all over the place. But Herja had proven she was better at this sort of sneaking thing than Penelope was over these last few weeks of training.

Inside, the bag was surprisingly bright. Penelope was further surprised that it was set up like a small cabin. Smooth walls formed three sides, while the floor and ceiling were carpeted. A jumble of blankets and pillows were strewn about, and lightstones were in the walls like windows.

Penelope barely felt the swaying of Herja's movements. Soon, the fabric edge opened, and Herja wormed her way inside.

"You've got a cozy setup here," Penelope said. There was just enough space to sit upright.

Herja tugged the fabric wall, pulling on the drawstrings to close it up. "I know, right? It's wonderful. Professor West, the fourth-year witch's professor, helped me assemble it. But we will need to be quiet; it doesn't fully block out any noise."

"And we won't suffocate?" Penelope asked worriedly. She pushed her pack into a corner.

"So long as we aren't dropped in water."

Penelope slumped against the wall. Great. That was one more thing to worry about. "And would we be crushed?"

"No. These walls are thick and sturdy. You could be jumping up and down on the bag, and we wouldn't even know." Herja reached into her pack and withdrew several books, as well as a slate, a piece of chalk, and some rags. "I figure it's going to be a very, very long trip. We're going to get bored."

Penelope smiled gratefully; then her smile faded as a thought struck her. A rising sense of horror left her embarrassed. "Uh-oh."

Herja hummed. "What is it?"

"What are we going to do for the bathroom?"

Herja opened her mouth, then her eyes widened. Her cheeks flushed as she put both hands over her mouth. "Oh, no. That's the one thing I didn't think about."

"Me neither. What are we going to do?"

Herja stared at her a moment longer, then giggled. She must be going crazy... but maybe it was kind of funny. They had this wonderful hiding place but the most basic of necessities...

"We'll figure something out," Penelope shrugged. "Let's think about it while we start a game."

CHAPTER
THIRTEEN

T he air was thick with the scent of decayed vegetation and stagnant waters. Luckily, the stench from the bogs had lessened of late. The manure smell no longer worked into every aspect of life... or maybe they were just getting used to it.

Wickham scrubbed the blood off his hands in a shallow pool, his stomach churning at the sight. He wasn't made for this sort of violence. He knew it was necessary for survival, but he'd never liked to take part in slaughtering farm animals.

It wasn't any better killing the rabbit he'd found. It wouldn't be much on its own, but as long as everyone else brought in something, they wouldn't go hungry... not tonight, at least.

"I can't understand how you can stand to touch it when it's dead," Adina said. She and Kaia were collecting allium on a small rise.

Wickham stuffed the rabbit into a bag. "How else are we going to feed ourselves? Your parents haven't done you any service by keeping you from knowing where meat comes from."

"I know that meat comes from dead animals. I just... haven't seen it happen up close. That scream..." she shuddered.

Adina went to rub her eyes, but Wickham caught her hand. "Careful, you'll irritate your eyes with your hands covered in the juice from the plants. It's like cutting an onion."

"I've never cut an onion," Adina admitted. "My parents thought I would be best suited to serve the Kingdom if I focused on education rather than the practical realities of life."

Kaia straightened and pushed her hair back. "I guess I can understand that if they thought you would lead a busy life in government. It's not very smart, though. You still need to know how to take care of yourself."

Adina snorted. "And now you understand why I don't want to be in the government at all."

Wickham dug a hole. "No, actually. I don't."

"You have to be willing to give it everything. Even things like cooking and cleaning are distractions from your most important work... my mother loves baking, but she hasn't baked for years because she never has the time."

"I never thought of it that way," Wickham said as he buried the inedible parts of the rabbit. "But now isn't the time we should think about this. We need to get back to the others. It's not safe out here."

"You're right," Adina shook herself. "I really shouldn't complain about this. I'm proud of my parents; I really am. I don't want to repeat myself over and over... they don't expect me to work in government, so why should I keep saying I don't?"

Kaia hummed as they headed back toward the others. "I don't think there's anything wrong with expressing yourself... so long as the people you're talking to have the right frame of mind to hear it. Wick is right, though. We shouldn't dwell on that right now."

Once they were back at camp, with the safety of Lee and the other students, Wickham produced the rabbit. Since he, Kaia, and Adina had left camp to gather food this time, they were given the night off from cooking. Icarus and Lena cooked instead while Jalene tidied camp.

Lee was on watch. He was always on watch since the first attack four days ago.

Wickham settled into his sleeping spot. They hadn't been able to salvage any bedding, but it was warm enough if they slept close enough to the fire.

Now that they were safe at camp, he could think about Adina's words some more. Did he resent becoming a witch because he didn't want to work in the government? No... he had never even considered government work. He'd always assumed he would graduate and go back home, find a job there...

Was that really the best use of his future, though? They did have a responsibility to the Kingdom. And yes, the Kingdom couldn't run without small farming communities like his home, but at the same time—

The crack of a twig made Wickham bolt upright. Before he could shout, Lee was in action. He roared out words that hurt Wickham's ears to hear. Flashes of light ran through the swamp, sending screams and shouts rising around them.

Wickham leaped to his feet and joined the others, huddled in a circle as they tried to peer into the gathering darkness. Movement here and there flitted in the shadows as Lee continued to send spell after spell.

As his heart pounded with terror, Wickham reached for Kaia's hand. She grabbed him, then reached to her other side and grabbed Adina's hand.

A surge of strength pulsed through Wickham. He willed a barrier to surround them. The sound of Lee's booming voice and the flashes of his spells filled all of Wickham's being. *Protection,* he thought. *A shield. Something to drive them away.*

Wind rushed in his face, and his eyes snapped open as his silvery hair blew back. A spinning, shining light hovered just above them, then suddenly exploded, sending shimmering lights all around them. Wickham gasped—

A dark shape flew from the bushes. It struck Lee in the temple and bounced away. The lights went out at once as he swayed, his eyes widening. Then his legs bent, and he crumpled to the ground.

"Lee!" Jalene screamed.

Lena put her hands over her ears. Icarus dropped to his knees next to their teacher, grabbing hold of Lee's shirt as though he could shake him awake.

The Odentian warriors, all wearing dark hoods and masks, emerged from the surrounding marshes. Wickham, Kaia, and Adina pressed closer together. Wickham's heart pounded in his ears, terror sweeping over him.

"What do you want?" Adina shouted. "Just leave us alone! Please!"

One of them, the leader with his plumed helmet, stepped forward. "Witches of Eldavon, my name is Finnegan of Odentia. Stand down, and no harm will come to you."

"Stand down?" Kaia burst out. "Do you see any weapons here? We have nothing to 'stand down' on. You're the same jerk who kidnapped us last year, too! What is *wrong* with you? Why are you so comfortable with continually attacking children?"

Finnegan's pale eyes zeroed in on her, and an irritated expression crossed his face. Wickham quickly pushed himself in front of his friend, worried that he might hurt her.

"You killed Lee," Lena whimpered. "You're going to kill us."

"He's breathing," Icarus said from where he knelt beside Lee. "It was a blunted arrow. He's alive, Lena. He's alive."

Wickham swallowed hard. He was alive for now, but he knew what damage even a blunt arrow could do to the skull. Human heads were surprisingly fragile, and nobody knew that better than a farm kid who had seen people get kicked by horses and cows. Even pigs! You never knew what damage was lurking beneath the surface of such a blow.

"See?" Finnegan said, gesturing to Icarus.

"You still attacked us," Kaia said.

Finnegan's hands clenched.

Before he could speak, though, a sudden high, whining noise pierced through the swamp. It was as though thousands of mosquitoes were converging on their location. Wickham's head swung around.

Adina's face was bright red, her lips slightly parted. At first, he thought the Odentian warriors had done something to her... until he felt the magic ripple through the air. All at once, insects rose from the surrounding swamp—thousands of them, enough to darken the sky.

The Odentian warriors shouted. They waved their hands about, slapping at the insects. More kept coming, going right for the warriors. The further they got from the students, the less intense the insects were buzzing.

Finnegan let out a frustrated yell, then choked as bugs flew into his mouth. Hacking and coughing, he stumbled away, bringing his warriors with him.

"Adina, that was brilliant!" Kaia gushed.

Wickham quickly went to where Icarus still knelt beside Lee. The professor's eyes were closed. His gums were still pink, thank goodness, but the spot on his temple where the blunted arrow had hit was already mottled purple.

"He's going to be all right, though," Icarus said, his voice high-pitched with worry. "He's only unconscious, right?"

"Head trauma is not something to mess around with. Blunted or not, it could still kill him." Wickham gently probed the area around the bruise. All the bones seemed in place. "The brain is like any other muscle; it can bruise and swell. But it's more delicate, and there's not much we can do about it."

Other than to screw a hole in Lee's head, Wickham thought to himself. But that would be a death sentence for sure. Wickham didn't have the medical knowledge to attempt surgery like that, even if he had the proper tools. And in a swamp like this?

"What can you do?" Jalene fretted.

Wickham shook his head, at a loss. Whenever Kassandra dealt with head injuries over the last year, the patient was awake. She had her magic spells to use. Wickham had nothing.

Adina cleared her throat. "We can't stay here, regardless. Let's get some long branches; we can use our jackets to make a stretcher. We can carry Lee with us as we go deeper into the swamp."

"Lena, Jalene, and I will get the branches," Kaia volunteered. "You three stay here and eat what you can. You should also go through all of what we have left and decide exactly what we can leave behind," she instructed.

Wickham hated the thought of leaving anything. He was only glad he'd left the beautiful herb box his family had given him at the Institute.

Darkness fell quickly over the swamp as the three girls left camp to find the right branches. They hadn't been gone long before Lee shuddered. At first, Wickham thought he was cold... but then he realized that the twitching and jerking was only on one half of the professor's body.

"He's seizing!" Wickham cried in dismay.

His mind raced as he desperately tried to find a way to help. There had to be something! Some mix of herbs...

Adina and Icarus knelt to either side of him, bombarding him with questions as his heart rate spiked. Wickham closed his eyes, forcing himself to block everything out. There was a boy in the village who had epilepsy. How did Kassandra treat those seizures?

The mixture of herbs she used sprang to mind instantly. But they were taken as a daily tea to prevent the seizures, not to help when one was already happening.

Better than nothing, he thought as he retreated to the fire. The stew was bubbling in the large pot over the fire. They had nothing else to use, so he dipped a bowl in, collecting only liquid, then set it down and sorted through his herb pouch.

"What do we do?" Adina demanded.

"Shut up and let me work!" Wickham roared back.

He sprinkled in the herbs, wishing he had rose petals—they were the only missing ingredient. Hopefully, that was for taste rather than anything else. But Kassandra always cast a spell over the tea, too...

Wickham placed his hands over the steaming bowl. He never knew the words Kassandra used, but spells were unique to their witches, weren't they?

The energy of the swamp seemed to pulse around him. He screwed his eyes shut as he whispered a prayer. *"Heal him."*

A spark seemed to light at his fingertips, but when he opened his eyes, nothing was there. The poor mix of herbs in stew broth bubbled, glowed, then returned to normal. Wickham's heart was in his throat as he continued to pray silently.

Lee was rigid from seizing, making it difficult for Wickham to get the spell into his mouth. Half of it spilled to either side of him until Wickham directed Adina to hold him down and Icarus to pry his mouth open.

After several tense moments, Lee's body relaxed. He grew still, and he let out a deep breath. Wickham collapsed into Icarus' side, unable to stop his own gasp of relief. The seizure had stopped, and from the sound of Lee's breathing, none of the potion had ended up in his lungs.

"Is he going to be okay?" Adina asked, her voice trembling.

"I don't know," Wickham replied exhaustedly. "You and Icarus should eat. I'll sit with him."

Icarus patted his back. "You should eat as well."

"I will. Soon," Wickham said.

He sat with their teacher, his arms wrapped around himself. Though the immediate danger had passed, this ordeal had just begun. The Odentian warriors were still out there. And they had no idea when help would come...

If it would come at all.

CHAPTER
FOURTEEN

Kaia's stomach rumbled. It was constantly rumbling these days. Since she had extra weight on her, she thought she would do better with the lack of food than the others... she even gave up her portions of the last meal they had to ensure there was enough for everyone.

Now, though, Kaia was so exhausted that even though she wasn't helping to carry Lee, she lagged the group.

"We need to stop for the night," she insisted.

Darkness was falling thick and fast around them. As it was, they would build their sleeping platforms in pitch black. With the Odentian warriors still out there, they didn't dare light a fire anymore.

It would be another cold, hungry night.

"She's right," Lena said. She directed the others to lower Lee to a semi-dry mossy spot on the ground. Then, she slumped against a tree and rubbed her arms. "Do you think we lost them this time?"

Finnegan and his warriors had caught up with them around noon the previous day. It had been four days since the initial attack that left Lee unconscious. The students were doing their best but could only find so much food in the swamp. They were nearly out of water entirely...

"Maybe we should surrender," Icarus said as he wearily sagged onto the ground. "Maybe if we do, Finnegan will help us. We'll have food and water and medicine for Lee."

"If they will give Lee medicine, they would have offered that already," Adina snapped. "If we surrender, they'll take us all prisoner and kill him."

Kaia drank the last drops of her precious water. They needed to find a stream, light a small fire, and boil enough to refill their water skins.

"We don't know they'll kill him," Icarus argued.

Adina put her hands on her hips. "Their help comes with too many strings. The Institute is the heart of our society, and they want to take us away from it. They want to steal us back to Odentia, where we'd never see our families again. Do you want that?"

Icarus flinched. "We don't know—"

"We do know it," Adina insisted. "We know it because they've already tried to kidnap us by force. And now they're doing it again. They wouldn't be coming at us with naked swords if they had good intentions."

Icarus bent his head, muttering under his breath.

"If they get their hands on magic, they'll go to war and try to conquer other kingdoms," Adina continued.

Wickham frowned. "Isn't it too much of an assumption to think that Odentia only wanted magic to perpetrate violence?"

Kaia ran a hand through her greasy hair. Well, she tried to, at least. Her fingers caught in the tangles and knots, making it impossible. "We haven't seen them for a while... maybe they've given up?"

"Or maybe," Lena said, "they're backing off to get us to retreat to the outer areas of the swamp, where they can grab us easier."

"What are we supposed to do, then?" Jalene snapped. "Continue just wandering around, getting ourselves more and more lost? We don't even have any water left! How is it better to die in this stupid swamp than surrendering to the Odentian warriors?"

"Spies, you mean," Adina muttered.

As they started to bicker and snap at each other, their voices grew louder. It wasn't even about what they were going to do next anymore. Adina called Lena names, Lena called Adina names, and Jalene called them both immature. Icarus insisted they were going to die. Wickham joined in, scolding everyone that they were acting like children; they needed to work together.

As hungry, tired, thirsty, cold, and afraid as they all were, Kaia didn't believe it was possible to work together... not right now, at least.

"I'm taking the pot to find water," she said. She dropped her makeshift pack and untangled the pot. "When I come back, I'm going to build a fire so we can boil the water and refill our water skins. I hope someone has found something to eat by then."

She turned on her heels.

"Wait," Adina called. "We can't go anywhere by ourselves."

Kaia looked over her shoulder, her gaze skimming over her fellow students. Who most needed to step back from the situation at hand? "Icarus. Will you come with me?"

Icarus opened his mouth, then closed it. He trailed after her, keeping close as they headed into the swamp. Kaia listened for the surrounding sounds, feeling out with her other senses as everything grew darker.

"Here," Icarus said suddenly.

Kaia could hardly see him but made her way over. He knelt beside a small puddle of water. It was just big enough to fill the pot. Good. At least they had water.

"It's probably unsafe to drink," Icarus said.

"That's why we'll boil it," Kaia replied, trying to keep her tone cheerful.

Icarus grunted as they carried the pot between them. "I still think our best shot is surrendering to the Odentian warriors."

"I understand why you would think that, but I also understand why Adina thinks her way, too." Kaia thought a moment, then shook her head. "In the end, none of us are thinking clearly right now. We won't be able to decide until we are physically in better condition."

"How can you always be so optimistic?" Icarus demanded, sounding both annoyed, exhausted, and envious.

Kaia squinted at his face, but there was so little light she couldn't see anything. It took all she had to keep moving along the path they'd taken. Kaia suddenly thought that maybe they were already lost and wouldn't find their way back to camp. But she pushed that aside. They hadn't gone terribly far.

Icarus grunted. "Well?"

"I'm not sure I'd call myself optimistic," Kaia said slowly. Her eyebrows furrowed. "I just don't like it when people fight. And so, I try my best to stop the fighting. I don't see how saying we need to eat, drink, and warm up before making any major decisions is optimistic, though."

She waited for a reply but got none. They fell into silence as they continued. They returned to camp soon enough, and Kaia was pleased to find a small fire already burning. She and Icarus placed the pot over it, and Icarus hunkered down, stretching his fingers to the flames.

Kaia sought Wickham. He crouched beside the still-unconscious Lee, looking worried. Though the students had done their best to keep their teacher clean and dry, the smell coming from his wound, a sure sign of infection, was becoming more noticeable.

"How is he doing?" Kaia asked Wickham.

"I don't know. There's no change that I can see, but I also don't know that much. I don't know if my spells are helping or hurting... they seem to help in the short term but look at how cracked his lips are. He needs more hydration."

Wickham squeezed a rag over the teacher's lips. This was the hardest part; they tried to keep giving him water but even a tablespoon too much could drown him. Lee needed help... professional help.

Help that was, right now, out of reach. What were they going to do?

THE NEXT MORNING, the students lit another fire and cooked up a mess of plants. They couldn't find any meat but collected edible bugs and grubs and threw them into the pot. Everyone was hungry enough that there were no complaints.

After they finished eating, Wickham wanted nothing more than to lie down and sleep. He was warm and full for the first time in days, the fire having baked off the constant, damp chill that had clung to him.

There was no time for rest, though.

"We need to pack up and get going again," Adina urged.

Icarus made an angry noise in his throat. "Just because your parents will be king and queen doesn't mean you get to tell us what to do."

"I'm not trying to tell you what to do—"

Kaia stood. "That's enough fighting! How are we supposed to work together when you two are at each other's throats?"

"So we should just pretend nothing's happening, like you?" Icarus snarled.

"Hey," Lena and Jalene said at the same time.

Wickham frowned. "There's no reason to be like that, Icarus."

The other boy looked at all of them, his hands tight in fists. He seemed to teeter on the brink of shouting, only to rock back on his heels and drop his head.

I wish Penelope and Herja were here. Penelope seemed to get people to listen to her with ease, and Herja was so smart, she would have figured something out by now... and that magic bookbag of hers would make it far easier to transport all their supplies and Lee.

But there wasn't any point in wishing they could be here when they weren't. They had to figure this out together.

"The way I see it," Kaia said warily, her eyes on Icarus. "We need to take a vote. We can keep going, we can surrender, we can camp here, we can try to make our way back out of the swamp. But after the vote, we must do what the group wants. Otherwise, we might as well not have a vote at all and just break apart, and each do our own thing."

Icarus scowled, folding his arms. "You mean I have to do what everyone else thinks is right."

"Or Adina, if we vote to surrender," Kaia said. She sounded exasperated. "This isn't about you, Icarus. It's about all of us."

Jalene nodded. "We vote on it. That's a good idea. That's what the adults do, so why shouldn't we?"

"I agree," Wickham nodded.

"All right," Icarus said, rubbing the back of his neck. "I think we should surrender. Who agrees with me?"

Nobody said anything. His scowl deepened as he glared at the forest floor.

"Does anyone think we should try to find our way out of the swamp?" Kaia asked.

Again, nobody replied.

"Who thinks we should stay here, then?" Adina said, sounding somewhat triumphant.

Wickham raised his hand. "All the bouncing around and carrying him isn't good for Lee. If we stay here, we can set traps and get better food, too."

"I think we should stay as well," Lena agreed.

Adina looked between Kaia and Jalene. Wickham met Kaia's eye, and she shook her head slightly.

"I think we should keep moving," Jalene said.

Kaia nodded.

Adina rolled her shoulders and straightened. "So that's three of us who want to keep moving, two who want to stay, and one who wants to leave. So, unless someone wants to change their vote, we move."

They stood in silence for a moment, waiting for someone to speak.

"No disagreements, so let's get ready to go," Adina said. "We still have a little fire left, so we should try to make another stew that we can eat while we're on the move. Is that agreeable to everyone?"

"It is for me," Kaia said.

"I'll go with you," Jalene volunteered.

They headed off, and Wickham returned to sit beside Lee. They had all slept well in the night—or as well as could be expected, at least. But Wickham had woken up constantly to drip water through Lee's lips. He didn't look any better, but at least he didn't look worse.

The group had made their decision. Wickham wasn't going to argue about staying, not now... but he had to wonder if he should have argued more when he voted to remain.

"Hold on, Lee," he whispered, checking his teacher's temperature. "Just hold on."

CHAPTER

FIFTEEN

P enelope frowned as she turned the slate upside down, hoping that a new perspective would help her figure out what exactly Herja had drawn. The other girl watched with a smirk, stretching out what space she could.

"A tree?" Penelope guessed.

"Nope! Guess again."

"A rock carved into a tree."

Herja burst into laughter and pressed her hand over her mouth to muffle it. "Really? A rock carved into a tree?"

"It looks like a tree to me!" Penelope turned the slate this way and that.

The two had gotten extremely bored over the last few days of travel, only opening the edge of the magical bag to get fresh air when they were in the air, swaying back and forth. They'd come up with this game a few hours ago—one was blindfolded and drew something, and the other had to guess.

"Is it a plant at all?" Penelope questioned.

"No, it's—" Herja cut off.

Penelope lowered the slate, her head turning toward their opening. The sounds of beating wings had died away, and movement shuffled around outside. The two of them moved to their knees, waiting. Though Penelope strained her ears, she couldn't hear any voices.

The bag suddenly jerked. It tipped upward, sending them sliding into the back wall. Herja started to call out, but Penelope put her hand over her mouth.

The drawstring, which looked far bigger on this side, opened, and the fabric fell aside, revealing a large, familiar face staring at them.

"Get out here. Now," Professor Farrow thundered.

They righted once more. Penelope and Herja glanced at each other, their eyes wide. "Oh, no," Herja whispered.

Penelope fought the insane urge to giggle. It wasn't like her to break the rules, and now to be exposed like this? She covered her face with her hands, fighting to regain control of herself. This wasn't good, and laughing would only make it worse!

Herja wormed her way out of the bag first, and Penelope followed. Luckily, one look at the furious expression on Professor Farrow's face killed any residual laughter.

Several dragons, humans, and witches stood in a circle around them. Penelope looked past them to see a thick jungle-like forest. A cool breeze wafted from this forest, bringing the musty scent of stale water.

"These are the Silent Marshes, aren't they?" she asked.

"Never mind that, Penelope." Professor Farrow put their hands on their hips; their silver eyes narrowed on the two girls. "What are you doing here? You were told to stay at the Institute."

Penelope felt Herja shift beside her, but this wasn't her idea—it was Penelope's, and Penelope would answer. "We came because we have friends in that marsh, and we're dragons. We're supposed to be protectors."

"You are going to cause us even more trouble," one human said, pointing accusingly at them. "We don't have the numbers to babysit you."

Herja shrugged. "Guess you won't babysit us, then. You'll just have to bring us with you."

Professor Farrow pinched the bridge of their nose. "You two are in massive amounts of trouble. No, don't say anything else. Go gather fire-wood, but stay in eyesight."

"I think we can—" Herja started.

"Now!" Farrow yelled.

Herja's eyes went as round as sauce plates. She grabbed Penelope's hand and scampered off. Once they were a few meters from the adults, they gathered sticks and logs.

"I've never seen Professor Farrow that angry," Herja whispered.

"Do you think we made a mistake?" Penelope asked, glancing nervously over her shoulder.

"I hope not."

They dawdled as they gathered the wood, reluctant to return. Occasionally, the raised voices of one or more of the adults reached them; it was clear they were arguing about what to do with Penelope and Herja.

After some time, they couldn't fit any more wood into their arms, and so they marched back. Penelope had every intention of going for more as soon as she dropped her armload at Professor Farrow's feet, but they held up a hand, stopping her.

"You will both be punished when we return to the Institute," they said, looking first at Penelope and then at Herja. "Regardless of where your hearts were, you've put us in a critical situation. We can't leave the swamp without everyone else. So, you'll stay with me as we continue our search."

Penelope let out a sigh of relief.

"We can use my bag to keep supplies, make it easier for us to keep moving," Herja volunteered, plucking it up from the ground. "And if we have bad weather, we can take refuge inside."

"Perhaps," Professor Farrow shook their head. "Go get some more wood again; we will camp here tonight, and tomorrow we'll split into groups and start the searches."

Penelope nodded once and led Herja away again. "So, what do you think?" she whispered. "Are we out of the woods?"

Herja glanced over her shoulder. "For now, yeah. I don't look forward to returning to the Institute, though."

"As long as we have Wickham, Kaia, and the others, I don't care how they punish us," Penelope said staunchly. "It's not like they're going to expel us."

"No... that's what worries me. What sort of punishment will we face?"

Penelope bent to gather more wood, ignoring the question. That didn't matter. They'd face it when it came. Right now, they had friends in need—and they were here to help. That was all that mattered.

THE NEXT MORNING, Professor Farrow woke Herja and Penelope before dawn and told them to gather their things. Herja quickly put everything together, stuffing her sleeping things into her bag. Penelope followed suit, and they added a whole barrel of water into it as well.

Herja waxed her black hair back from her face with the honeycomb paste she had brought. Penelope braided hers, then pinned it into a bun and cemented it in place with the honeycomb paste.

"We are going into hostile territory," Professor Farrow explained. "As such, you will call me Row while we are here. Even in your minds —you may not think it makes much difference, but a few seconds can change everything."

"Understood," Herja said. *Row, row, row.*

Your boat, gently down the stream—

She shook the song from her mind and focused on Row.

"You will obey my every command the moment I tell you, no matter what," Row continued. Their silver eyes narrowed as they focused on Penelope. *"No matter what."*

Penelope nodded. "Understood, Prof—Row."

Row tapped her forehead. "That's why you need to think of me as Row now."

"Yes, Row," Penelope said. She wore a sleeveless tunic today, her muscular arms making Herja feel inadequate—maybe she should focus on building her strength more.

"We should have weapons," Herja said, pushing that from her mind as well—no point in dwelling on what she couldn't change in the next five minutes.

Row shook their head, a thunderous look coming to their face again. "Absolutely not."

"But—" Herja cut herself off. Row said everything must be obeyed, no matter what. Did that include this?

As she puzzled over how much of a fuss she could reasonably raise, Row's expression softened. They sighed as they ran a hand through their hair. "You don't have weapons training yet. Even if you did, the moment you have a weapon in your hand, you become a deadly threat to the enemy."

"As dragons, aren't we a threat already?" Herja asked hesitantly.

"Right now, you're both inexperienced dragons who can't even shift yet. You're valuable as a potential resource," Row explained. "I would like to keep it that way. The only reason I'm letting you come at all is that you'd be vulnerable here by yourselves, and I've gotten to know you, Herja. You'll get yourself in trouble on your own terms... but you are also resourceful, which might be useful."

Herja didn't think much of that, but she shrugged it off. Row had a point, after all.

"Look for any footprints, any trace of human passage," Row instructed them as they headed into the swamp. "Be vigilant and let me know if you see anything."

Herja nodded as she focused on the surrounding ground. Within a few moments, however, she realized she didn't have a prayer at helping with the tracking. She could barely discern where Row was walking, and they were only a few feet in front of her.

Then I'll use my eyes to look out for other things, Herja told herself, lifting her head to observe the swamp.

The trees that grew here were twisted, dense, and small. They grew together, packed as though someone had gone through the planted them in the shadows of each other, deliberately making them shaped a certain way.

"Row," Penelope called. "I smell smoke."

Herja sniffed the air but only smelled that strange scent that reminded her of the dirt basement of the new orphanage house as it was being built. Row took Penelope at her word and fell back to her position.

"This way," Penelope said, pointing.

"How can you tell?" Herja asked.

Penelope picked her way through leafy bushes. "I've lived with the Fire Watch my whole life."

They soon came to the dead coals of a campfire. They were cold, but the ashy scent was still there if Herja bent close and sniffed. Penelope had to have a great nose on her.

Maybe I shouldn't try to be the best at everything. Herja thought. *Maybe I shouldn't even try to be great at everything. Maybe what I should do is learn how to recognize and use other people's strengths.*

Row bent over something on the ground. Herja silently joined them, soon catching sight of a thin, glittering, thread-like line.

"Stay behind me," Row warned as they followed the line. Herja stuck close to Row's heels while Penelope took up the rear.

Through wild raspberry bushes, and up a small hill, they came to the end of the thread. A man wearing Odentian armor slumped against a tree. The strand of glistening thread crisscrossed over his body so many times that he looked like someone had wrapped him up in cobwebs and stuck him against the tree.

"Is he dead?" Penelope gasped.

At the sound of her voice, the man's head popped up. His eyes were glazed, but otherwise, he looked perfectly healthy.

"Hullo!" he called cheerfully. "Are you here for the performance as well?"

"Performance?" Herja asked.

The Odentian warrior nodded, beaming peacefully. "Oh, yes. The funny little glowing people come here and put on a wonderful show. Then, they give me kisses and feed me and go away again. It's quite fun."

"You came to kidnap Eldavon witches, though," Row said, crouching beside the warrior.

"Oh, yes, we did. But I don't want to anymore. I'd rather stay here. It's so peaceful...." His head drooped back to his chest, and he let out a satisfied sigh as he fell back asleep.

Row gestured for the girls to go back the way they came. "A nymph nest. They must be feeding off his sweat... We're on the right track, at least."

"Is he going to be okay?" Penelope asked, her brow puckered. "Shouldn't we free him?"

"No. Right now, he's harmless and confined. Nymphs don't kill people, so he's safe, as well. We'll collect him on our way back," Row said.

They found the path again, and they started moving through the swamp. Herja searched the tree and bushes and kept her ears sharp for any unusual sounds. She soon realized why this place was called the Silent Marshes. Every sound seemed to be dampened, coming from a distance—even her own breathing.

"I hope we find them soon," Penelope whispered beside her. "This place is eerie."

"Faster," Row said, picking up the pace. "They'll have moved closer to the center of the swamp. Lee's smart enough to use his advantage of knowing the locale. I want to get into the bogs before nightfall."

Herja's heart sank. Bogs. Maybe she hadn't thought this through after all.

CHAPTER

SIXTEEN

K aia scratched the large bug bites on her arms. The bugs had
been terrible today; she had thought that the bright sun
above them would get too hot for the insects, but as it turned
out, it only encouraged them.

"I wish Nolen were here," she sighed.

"Nolen?" Icarus, her buddy on their search for food, questioned.

"He's one dragon in our year. On our journey to the Silver Springs,
he found plants that drove away the bugs. Remember?"

Icarus frowned. "I guess maybe a bit. He was the sour-looking kid,
right? Like there was a cloud of thunder over his head all the time?"

Kaia smacked his arm lightly. "He wasn't sour-looking at tall. Sure,
he was serious, but that's not bad."

"We should head back to the others," Icarus said, sounding cross. "I
don't think there's anything to find here."

"We still have half an hour before we need to head back."

Icarus shook his head. "I'm too tired for this. I want to go back."

Kaia could understand his exhaustion. Her arms still ached from
carrying the stretcher today, and Icarus had insisted on carrying all
day. She ought to have suggested someone else come out looking for
food with her.

"Okay, let's head back to camp," she said, turning.

"I just have to use the bathroom first," Icarus said.

Kaia nodded.

"Don't wait for me."

"I have to; I don't want to be caught on my own," Kaia said. Besides, she needed to relieve herself as well. That seemed like a slightly less important reason to keep close by, though.

Icarus headed off in one direction, Kaia going in the other. She dug a hole to do her business in, then covered up the hole. She couldn't wait to get back to the Institute... the pit toilets had been bad enough, but if this kept up, she would surely get an infection!

"Icarus?" she called as she returned to the path.

Silence answered her.

"Icarus?" A chill crawled up her spine. What if the Odentian warriors had found him? "Icarus, answer me!"

Still nothing.

Panic taking a firmer hold on her, Kaia crashed through the foliage on the other side of the path, where Icarus had gone. She called out again and again until she suddenly stumbled on another open path.

Icarus bent over the dirt, intent on doing something. He didn't seem to have heard Kaia, which was ridiculous considering how loudly she'd been calling.

Her relief at finding him soon came to an abrupt halt as she got closer, and his actions became clear. He was arranging a series of rocks in an arrow... light stones that would show up clearly at night.

"What are you doing?" Kaia demanded.

Icarus jumped, yelping. He whirled, his fists lifting as though he planned to punch her. Kaia flinched away from him, her eyes widening.

"Don't sneak up on me!" Icarus shouted. He shifted to one side like he was trying to hide his 'artwork.'

"What are you doing?" Kaia asked again. She sidestepped and pointed to the arrow. "What is that? How many light stones do you have? Don't you know that will show the Odentian warriors exactly where we are?"

Icarus stepped back. "No. I'm leaving a trail for the Institute. They'll never be able to find us if we don't leave something for them to find."

"Except for magic," Kaia argued. She put her hands on her hips. "And why haven't you told anyone? We would have told you it was a bad idea. No wonder the Odentian warriors keep finding us! You're leading them right to us!"

A guilty look came onto Icarus' face, but it quickly disappeared. "You don't know what you're talking about."

Oh, but she did. She understood far more than he realized. Kaia fell back another step. He'd been the one who insisted that they should surrender to the Odentian warriors. He was the one who had been with Adina during that first attack.

Horror rose in Kaia's throat, choking off her words.

"Look, I just think we need to be doing something other than racing deeper and deeper into this swamp. It's not helping anyone," Icarus continued. The anger was draining from his face, an anxious expression replacing it. "Kaia, you have to understand—"

"I understand that you decided that you know best, and that you were going to betray us all, even after our vote," Kaia said, finding her voice again. "We're going back to camp, and you'll tell them everything."

She started to bend to grab the light stones, but Icarus grabbed her arm to stop her. "You can't do that!"

"Let go of me," Kaia snarled, twisting her arm this way and that.

"You can't tell them," Icarus repeated. "Please!"

"Why not?"

Icarus opened his mouth and closed it several times. His shoulders slumped forward, and he let out a heavy, defeated sigh. "I'm not doing this because I think I know better than our group. I'm trying to do what's best for Eldavon and Odentia both."

"How is this—"

"If you'll just let me talk, I will tell you," Icarus insisted.

Kaia's nostrils flared. She finally twisted herself free from Icarus' grasp and nodded curtly. She'd listen to what he had to say, even though she couldn't believe he'd have a good reason for this betrayal.

All the same... she hoped he did.

"My parents are from Odentia," he said, spreading his hands before him as though offering the reason physically. "They've talked about how terrible life was there, how hard it was to get away, and how much better life is here."

Kaia shifted from foot to foot. "I know about that. It's awful but how will kidnapping Adina help with that?"

Icarus closed his eyes briefly. "The adults only see what they want to see. Odentia has a new king. A king who wants to make change... but he can't. Not without magic."

"Odentia doesn't have a new king."

"It does," Icarus insisted. "They told me. He hasn't been announced yet because they're afraid people will try to assassinate him because of his new policies. They want to make changes, Kaia. Don't you see? If we can give them magic, their lives will be better."

Kaia turned away, massaging her temples. If it were true Odentia had a new king who was trying to improve their social infrastructure, then magic would help them. Life was hard, and Odentia had suffered several years with poor crops...

But magic won't fix their problems when they keep turning good farmland into private land, Kaia thought, remembering something she had overheard her parents saying.

"The problem with Odentia is that they think magic will fix their problems putting no effort into it," Kaia said slowly. "The problem is that they have enough food for everyone, but a small population hordes all the best foods and leaves the rest of the people to get by on turnips."

"You're only repeating what you've heard. You don't know for certain."

"And you're only repeating what you heard," Kaia replied.

She tugged at her knotted silver hair.

Even though she was still furious at Icarus for betraying them, she must admit she empathized with his reasons. It had to be terrible, hearing about how awful things were in his parents' home country and being unable to do anything to improve the situation.

"I understand why you are doing this," she finally said, turning to Icarus. Her limbs dragged toward the ground, and she could hardly keep herself standing straight. "And I think you're a good person for wanting to help them, especially when you've never met them before."

"So, you agree?" Icarus stepped forward.

Kaia shook her head. "I don't agree. Not at all. If this new king was really determined to make positive changes, why wouldn't he ask for help? Why steal it?"

"He thinks..." Icarus trailed off.

"Eldavon has offered Odentia real aid," Kaia continued. "I was at the palace this summer; I heard many things. I know we offered them plenty of food, we offered to send knowledgeable farmers, and we offered to give them herds of animals. Odentia refused it all."

Icarus shook his head. "No. No, you're wrong."

"Maybe they do feel desperate," Kaia said.

"They do."

"Maybe they're so used to the ways their own court runs things they're unable to understand offers of help can come without strings," she continued, softening her tone. "I don't know. But I know that kidnapping Adina and the rest of us isn't the way to do it. If Odentia will resort to stealing a child away from her home, using trickery and violence to get what they want, how can we trust them to use magic for good?"

Icarus turned his face to the sky. A glint of moisture pooled in the corners of his eyes, but Kaia pretended not to see.

"They will use it for good, however. Don't you see? The sun and moon and earth gifted this to us for the good of the entire world, not just Eldavon."

Kaia nodded slowly. The stories were straightforward about that. "You're right... and that means we must change our ways somehow, too. But this?" Kaia pointed at the light stones. "Betraying us? Putting us on a violent path? It's not the way."

"I... all right. I'll stop. I promise. Just please, don't tell anyone."

Kaia's stomach clenched. There was only one thing here that she knew, and that was that she had to tell the others. But would Icarus try to run if she told him that? Would he attack her? He had already broken her trust; she wasn't sure how far he would go...

She made herself smile. "Of course. Let's just get back to the group. We can say we found the light stones on the path."

Icarus smiled back at her, the relief clear on his face. Kaia quickly gathered up the light stones he'd put on the path, hiding her face from him. She wasn't much of a liar and didn't want him to see the truth in her eyes.

"It was this way, right?" she said, gesturing once she had gathered the stones.

"Yeah," Icarus replied.

They headed through the foliage close together. Darkness dropped around them rapidly. What she hated most about this place was how quickly the night came on them. Day came just as quickly, going from pitch darkness to bright light in a matter of minutes, but it was just... spooky.

She pulled a light stone out to glow on their path and came to the little camp the others had set up. A tiny fire burned in a pit in the center of a grove of trees, down out of sight from the surrounding area. The pot was placed over this, the water inside boiling.

"What do you have there?" Wickham asked as they drew closer.

Kaia opened her fist to reveal the light stone. It was slightly warmed by her hand.

"We found some on the path," Icarus lied smoothly. "Isn't it great? If we put them in the fire, we'll be able to stay warmer with a smaller fire."

Wickham drew closer. Kaia could see his eyes were wide with hope in the light from the stone. A smile blossomed over his face.

When faced with impossible choices, people do desperate things. Kaia could understand how Icarus thought he was doing what was best. She could understand how he could be manipulated. He'd have no reason to distrust the people who came to him, begging for help.

Impossible choices. But she already knew what her answer to it would be.

"We didn't find them on the path," she said as Icarus kept talking about what they could do with the 'discovered' light stones. She clenched her fist over the one she held and turned.

His expression was startled, his breathing rapid.

"He was marking the trail," she said, her voice shaking as she revealed the truth. "He was showing the Odentian warriors which way he went. He was leading them right to us."

CHAPTER
SEVENTEEN

Icarus shouted and shoved Kaia from behind. Wickham caught her as she stumbled, and quickly put himself between her and the other boy.

As he braced himself, Wickham noticed how much shorter and slighter he was. Icarus could seriously hurt him. But Icarus wasn't even looking at him; his gaze was focused on Kaia.

"You said you wouldn't tell! You promised!"

Kaia cleared her throat audibly. When she spoke, her voice shook. "I'm sorry. I didn't... it's that I couldn't... I'm sorry."

"You lied to me," Icarus seethed. He started forward and Wickham drew himself up as big as he could make himself and held out both hands.

"Stop," Adina said.

Kaia skirted around Wickham. "I am sorry, Icarus. If I could believe you wouldn't keep doing it, I wouldn't have said anything. But they deserve to know everything. They—"

"I hate you," Icarus seethed. "I HATE YOU!"

"Hey," Wickham snapped, unable to stop himself. "You were the one leading those warriors to us... how long have you been doing it?"

He could hardly believe what Kaia said, but Icarus had all too willingly admitted the truth of it. "Is it your fault that Lee is like this!?"

Icarus flinched.

Anger swept through Wickham's body. He'd never considered himself a violent person. But right now, he had to fight back the urge to punch Icarus in the face. It was his fault. He'd led the Odentian warriors and now Lee might die.

"You're supposed to be our friend," Lena cried. "How could you do this to us?"

"I didn't—" Icarus protested.

Jalene crowded him from the other side. "You traitor!"

"He did. But he has a reason," Kaia said. It was as though she was trying to defend him now. Wickham stared at her, trying to figure it out. Why would she want to defend Icarus after revealing the truth of his actions?

The other three witches ignored both Kaia and Wickham, focusing instead on Icarus. Adina stepped in front of him, staring him in the eyes.

"Why should we keep you around, then? If you're going to betray us and our Kingdom, why shouldn't we force you out of our group and let you to go surrender yourself to them like you want?" she snarled.

Wickham shuddered at her words. He stepped forward, ready to insert himself into the situation when Icarus dropped to his knees.

"Please," he begged. "Please listen to me. I didn't mean for anyone to get hurt."

"Why should we—" Adina started.

Kaia grabbed her elbow, stopping her. "Because regardless of his actions, he is still a witch. He did what he did because he thought he was working toward a better future. We don't condemn people without hearing their side of the story."

Adina opened her mouth again, then shut it. A look crossed over her face, and she retreated, turning her back to the group.

The tension in the group was so thick it could strangle them all. Wickham cleared his throat, bringing the attention to him. "Kaia is right. Even though I don't want to listen to Icarus, he does deserve the right to state his point of view before we decide what to do. But before we do that, we ought to get some food."

"We didn't find anything," Kaia admitted.

Wickham shook his head. "Then we'll use the rest of my herbs to flavor the water and we'll add more of these marsh weeds. It'll fill our stomachs, if nothing else."

Adina turned back. "Not all your herbs. Keep enough for Lee aside."

"I will."

The water was already boiling, so Lena and Jalene gathered weeds to throw into the pot along with the herbs Wickham could spare. He made up another small potion for Lee; the teacher wasn't showing any signs of recovery even now. If anything, he was getting worse.

Once they were eating, Icarus told his story, the same as he'd told Kaia. Wickham's heart ached as Icarus detailed the horrible things his parents had gone through before they came to Eldavon.

Once he was finished, he handed his portion of the food to put back into the pot. "And that's why I did it. Because I want to help, and I thought this was the best way I could."

Wickham poked at his weed stew. It tasted horrible, but at least it was hot and filled his stomach. Now that he'd heard Icarus' argument laid out like that, he didn't understand why Eldavon would deny Odentian magic.

"Maybe..." Wickam hesitated. "Maybe we could listen to what Finnegan has to say? We could—"

"No," Adina said.

"But if we could get help from them, it would prove that they were telling Icarus the truth," Wickham argued. "They could have used a real arrow against Lee, but they used a blunted one."

"And with their knowledge, there's no way Finnegan wouldn't know exactly what he was doing," Adina insisted.

"Yeah, he probably did it on purpose to force us to turn to him for help," Jalene said.

Lena stuck the end of a stick into the fire. "But at this point, do we have a choice? We're eating weeds! Lee is dying... if we could get any sort of help, isn't it worth staying alive?"

Adina opened her mouth, then closed it again. She hunched her shoulders and stared into her bowl.

"That's assuming that Finnegan would actually help us," Kaia murmured.

Wickham turned to her, relieved that she was finally talking once more. "What do you mean?"

"Let's look at the situation like this," Kaia said, spreading her hands out on her knees. "Finnegan attacked our camp. He destroyed our supplies and attempted to kidnap Adina already. All we did was be here, and he came at us with violence. How can we trust someone who does that?"

Wickham rubbed his hands over his face. "I'm not sure we really have a choice anymore, Kaia. Look at us. We're in over our heads. This isn't like when we were waylaid at the Silver Springs. We don't have people coming to save us. We don't even know if they know we're missing."

"And we all know we're supposed to serve the Kingdom, to protect its people, right?" Kaia said, finally looking up.

There were a few nods, but most of the group just watched her with furrowed eyebrows. A sickening feeling filled Wickham's stomach. He had a horrible premonition that he knew exactly what Kaia was going to get at.

"Finnegan's help doesn't come without strings. He will give us food and water and stop hunting us, but it means giving ourselves up to Odentia. Giving them magic," she added, her voice lowering. "How can we trust they won't misuse our magic? How can we believe they won't do even worse things, to force us to break our morals?"

Lena shook her head. "What could they do, though?"

"Don't you remember how they starved us when we were captured at the Silver Springs?" Adina asked.

"You just heard of how Icarus' family was treated; and they weren't even doing anything," Kaia added. "Odentia isn't like here. They're so different."

"Should we take a vote on it?" Adina asked, looking around.

Wickham's lips twitched humorlessly. "I was going to say no, but I think we should. Everyone lay out an idea and then we can vote. More than just one person stating our options."

Adina and Kaia both nodded at him.

"I'll start," Wickham said, straightening. "We make camp here. Best to stay in one place, near water and something like food. We make ourselves a shelter and build up some sort of wall around us. Lena?"

She was sitting next to him. She chewed her lip a moment before she brushed her hair over her shoulder. "We split up. We all go our own ways and try to get out of the swamp by ourselves."

Next was Jalene, who offered, "We keep moving, but we try to make our way out of the swamp now, rather than going deeper and deeper into it. We retrace our steps and hope that the Odentian warriors don't expect it."

"I... surrender," Icarus murmured. "We hand ourselves over to Finnegan and get his help."

Adina stared deep into the fire, her hands were fists. "You all continue going and I turn myself over to Finnegan and hope he stops hunting you."

Wickham flinched; it was an option they were all thinking; he knew that. He hated hearing it out loud, though.

Last of all was Kaia. She filled her bowl with a second helping of the stewed weeds. "We tie Icarus to the stretcher so he can't run away and tell the Odentian warriors where we are, and we travel some more. We use the light stones to light our way at night and we just keep going until we're at the other side, or we drop from exhaustion."

"Let's vote on it," Adina said, her voice shaking. "Those in favor of staying?"

Wickham raised his hand. Jalene and Lena did as well.

"Split up?" Adina continued.

Nobody.

"Surrender?"

No votes.

Adina swallowed. "Turn me over?"

Again, no hands lifted.

"We continue day and night with Icarus tied up?" Adina continued after a slight pause.

Kaia shook her head, hunching deeper into herself. Nobody else lifted their hands.

Then there was only one last thing. "Then, who all says we retrace our steps and try to get out of the swamp?"

Kaia and Adina lifted their hands.

"What about you?" Lena asked, nudging Icarus with her toes.

Icarus lifted his head. "I rescind my right to vote... since I acted without good faith earlier..."

A heavy weight settled on Wickham's shoulders. That meant with only five votes, they were going to stay in this spot. Although he knew it would be easier on Lee, he also understood Finnegan would have an easier time finding them now.

"We camp here, then," Adina confirmed. She rested her elbows on her knees. "Now what do we do with Icarus?"

"You can tie me to the stretcher, like Kaia suggested," Icarus said. "I... I still don't know if what I did was wrong, but I understand you can't trust me."

It was such a flip from his behavior and accusations at Kaia before they ate Wickham wasn't sure if he could trust this repentant version of Icarus. He wished he could... keeping a fellow student as a prisoner made his skin crawl.

But what choice did they have?

"I'll take charge of him," Wickham volunteered. "Since I'm the other boy here, I'll take him away from camp to do his business and all that."

Jalene looked Wickham up and down, then Icarus up and down. "He's a lot bigger than you. Do you think you can handle him?"

Wickham shoved the gross weed stew into his mouth again. Though it made him gag, he didn't have much choice. It tasted better cold, somehow, rather than hot. "I don't think we have a choice, do we?"

"We really don't," Lena said.

Adina rubbed her eyes. "Alright. So that's decided. Now someone else decide what we're going to do first to make this place a decent camp. I can't think anymore and I'm about to start bawling my eyes out so I'd like a little privacy, please."

She stood, tipping her stew over, and headed just outside of camp. Wickham would have warned her not to go too far, but as soon as she was out of sight, he heard her sobbing.

Lena was the first to speak. "We have a water source; we can't really do anything tonight, so our first order of business will be to make sure we're all warm enough to sleep. Tomorrow, we can divide into two groups... one can start building shelter and walls while the other can gather food."

There was a murmur of agreement from the others. Wickham finished his stew, then filled his bowl with the watery broth that had developed. This he took back to Lee and started the painstaking task of sponging water into his mouth.

Sun bless us, Moon protect us, he prayed. *We need help.*

CHAPTER

EIGHTEEN

A sharp pain in the back of Herja's neck made her slap at the spot. Her hand hit something larger than she expected and she whirled, crying out.

A creature buzzed at eye-level. It was the size of a hummingbird, with feathery wings beating just as rapidly attached to a tiny humanoid body. It clutched a tiny spear in its hands. Herja blinked.

"A brownie just attacked me," she called over her shoulder.

Penelope turned back. "A brownie? But they don't attack people, they're peaceful and—Ouch!"

Another brownie had dived from the canopy, hurling a spear at her head. It stuck into her scalp. As Herja turned to help her, the one that had already attacked her came again, jabbing its spear at her ear. Herja cried out, covering her ears, then her eyes as more brownies came out of the bushes, attacking.

"Hold still," Row shouted.

Herja could hardly hear them over the sounds of the buzzing wings. She dropped to her knees, trying to protect her face with one hand while batting at the brownies with the other. Dozens of spears stabbed through her skin, leaving behind an excruciating pain.

"Halb," Penelope moaned.

Herja risked looking up long enough to see her standing there, a spear hanging out of her lower lip.

"I cab feel my lib."

With horror, Herja felt a numbness spreading from the tips of the brownies' spears. They must be poisoned!

"Go away!" Herja shouted, returning to her efforts to bat them away. It only seemed to incense the brownies further. They chirped to one another and started formations to dive bomb the girls.

Row grabbed Herja's hand. They pulled her and Penelope in, shielding both girls with their body while also stopping them from attacking the brownies. Penelope blubbered something unintelligible, but Row hissed at her to be quiet.

"Be utterly still," they said. "And try to match my pitch. Brownies communicate in song, we show we aren't a threat."

Row hummed. It was a low, deep sound that Herja already knew she couldn't match. She tried anyway, feeling the vibrations rumble in her throat almost painfully. It reverberated in her chest, a growing growl that was at once a song and a thunder. The swamp seemed to grow warmer as she did so.

The sharp stabbings of pain were along her back now, along with that numbness that frightened her more than the pain did.

Penelope whimpered and Herja squeezed her hand tighter. Both girls closed their eyes and tried to match Row's humming. Slowly, the frenzied attacks lessened, then disappeared altogether. Part of Herja wondered if she had just grown utterly numb to it all, but she had to hope that wasn't the case.

The whirling, fluttering of their wings faded slightly. Row kept Herja and Penelope down for a moment longer before slowly letting them up. Great welts ran along all of their exposed skin and Penelope's lip and cheek were swollen terribly.

The brownies didn't move to attack again, though.

Row took the girls by the hands and led them backwards, toward the path again. The brownies hovered closer, following them as they moved away. Once they were through the bushes, though, the noise from the brownies cut out entirely.

"We should be alright now," Row said. Their voice was rougher than normal, like their throat was raw.

Herja's own throat ached now that she had stopped humming. She rubbed her neck, wincing as her fingers caught one of those tiny spears.

"Let's get some mud on these stings," Row continued. "It's the only thing that helps with brownie venom."

Herja nodded, feeling the swelling on her neck. It didn't seem to get worse, but the numbness was draining away again, and it *hurt*.

"I thought brownies were supposed to be a docile magical species," she said to distract herself from her current physical state.

Poor Penelope could only nod, her lips swollen so bad it had to hurt just to move them.

"They are," Row replied. They led the girls through the bushes into a shallow pool, almost as though they had known it would be there. They scooped up the mud and apply it to their arms.

Herja and Penelope followed suit.

"It has to be the Odentian warriors, then," Herja said as she worked. "They must have upset the brownies somehow. Maybe they destroyed a nest or something."

"It could be," Row agreed. "On the other hand, it might be something that the students did. We don't know and there isn't any point in jumping to conclusions. What we do is decipher what information we need to take from this, not go assigning blame."

"And wub do we neeb to take from dis?" Penelope asked laboriously.

"That the swamp has been disturbed. That the natural balances are upset, and so we need to be wary and alert." Row rocked back on their heels and helped Penelope apply mud to her face. "And that it's important to understand what might cause a creature to attack, and how to defend yourself."

"You mean, without attacking them back?" Herja asked. Her nose scrunched up as she tried to decipher the lesson.

Row shook their head. "It's important to know when you don't need to defend violently and when there are no other options. But no matter what you face, you must always remember to hold on to compassion, no matter what else."

"I don't think those brownies were showing us much compassion," Herja groused.

"But did they think we were attacking them without provocation? Once we established we weren't a threat, they stopped attacking... isn't that compassion?" Row arched a single eyebrow at her.

Herja shrugged, not ready to give up on that one just yet.

Penelope seemed to have a better grasp on what Row was getting at, though. She asked, "Does that mean we should have compassion for the Odentian warriors?"

She was certainly speaking clearer. In fact, the swelling on her face had gone down by at least half. Herja probed one of her own brownie-welts. It was still painful, but only that of a horsefly's bite.

"We should. Cautiously," Row said. They stood and scanned the swamp, then picked a direction.

Herja sighed. More walking. After the ordeal with the brownies, part of her wanted to just curl up and sleep. But Wickham and Kaia were out there, along with the other witches. They must be terrified. The sooner she, Penelope and Row found them, the sooner they could all get back to the Institute.

"Why do you say cautiously?" Penelope asked.

Row glanced at her. Their normally stoic expression softened. "Because it's too easy to believe Odentia is more similar to Eldavon than it is. You're still young; you don't fully understand yet how different a culture can be. How different it is to live under a single ruler who believes they were born with the right to rule, rather than elected rulers who view it to serve the people."

Herja trailed a little behind. She didn't think that it was her right to rule... did she? She would be Queen one day to help others. It was her responsibility.

She would not make Eldavon a worse place to live, right? She'd be a good Queen... wouldn't she?

PENELOPE COULDN'T STOP THINKING about what Row said about Eldavon having a much different culture than Odentia. She hadn't ever considered that before. How could they be so different?

"Is it because we have magic?" she asked after some time.

Row glanced at her, seeming to understand this was a continuation of their previous conversation. "I can't answer that. I don't know enough of Odentia's history. It could be the magic. Maybe the first dragons, witches, and humans insisted they use their magic for good... All I really know is that Odentia considers those who don't have magic to be human, and say that we think of them as less than because we say humans have their own magic."

Penelope frowned. "But humans do have magic."

"They don't see it. They see dragons and witches as magic and that's it."

"But that doesn't even make any sense," Penelope protested.

Herja, who had been behind them, spoke up. "Only because you've been taught that humans have magic, too, just a different sort. Whereas they don't believe there is any other magic. Is that right?"

Row nodded at her with a slight smile.

They continued, finding evidence here and there that the students had passed through this way. They had no way of knowing how far they'd gone from here, though Row said they were getting closer. How did they know, though?

When dusk fell, Row gave them each a light stone. "We'll continue on until midnight," they said.

Herja nodded and Penelope drank more from her waterskin. She understood now why the adults said she and Herja would slow them down... she wished they could start camp. But she was here now, and she would not slow Row down any more than she already had.

Once midnight hit, Row called a stop and told them to rest. Herja and Penelope bedded down at once, but Row stepped through the bushes. Penelope rolled over, pressing her side against Herja's. The night was chilly and having the warmth from her friend made her feel a little less alone.

"Penelope?"

"Yeah?"

"Are you sleeping?"

Penelope pillowed her head on her arm. "No. We should try to rest, though. It won't be that long until Row wants to get moving again. I saw tracks earlier there were too big for the students. If they came through here, the Odentian warriors can't have been far behind."

"I don't think I can sleep."

Penelope reached out to pat Herja's head in the darkness. "I understand, but we have to try. Would you like to sleep in the book bag? I know the forest can be frightening in the dark."

Herja rolled over. There was just enough moonlight that Penelope could see her outlined against the deeper black of the swamp. "That's not why I can't sleep. I just keep thinking about Row said, about compassion."

Penelope frowned. "Why?"

"I... I don't think I have enough compassion. It's not something you can learn, either, is it? I mean, I keep thinking about how when we were going up to the Silver Springs, you just sort of stepped in and took the leadership role, and made sure we didn't leave anyone behind. I never would have done that."

"I'm used to moving in large groups and working on getting everyone to move together, though," Penelope replied. "You're used to pushing yourself and yourself alone. I don't think you lack compassion... maybe you just lack experience at being compassionate."

Herja sighed as she rolled onto her back again. "I just... I don't know. There's that and then there's... well what sort of lives do the people of Odentia really have?"

Penelope hugged her friend. "You're letting your mind run away with you. There's nothing we can do about any of that right now. We need to focus on the mission."

"The mission. You're right." Herja rolled once more, her back to Penelope. "Thank you. We should try to rest now."

Penelope rolled so her back was to Herja, too. But once the sound of their voices was gone, the silence of the swamp pressed in deeper on her. Now Penelope wondered what their lives in Odentia were like. What would drive grown adults to attack children?

And what punishments faced them in their homes if they failed on their mission?

CHAPTER

NINETEEN

Kaia sensed something was amiss in the early morning hours. The prickling on her neck and arms woke her, and she bolted upright with a gasp. Everything was still just dark enough that she couldn't tell what was around her.

But then someone doused the flames of their small fire, sending red sparks into the air, and Kaia knew. The Odentian warriors had found them.

Her mind raced. They should have left. They should have built better defenses. They should have—

She screamed. Heart pounding, she screamed simply to wake everyone else up. Cries rose around the camp, followed by a strange metallic rasping noise.

It wasn't until a sword was laid across her neck and Finnegan's voice boomed out for her to shut up that she realized the warriors were unsheathing their swords.

This couldn't be real. Even as cruel as Finnegan had been, he couldn't really have a sword against her neck, could he? Kaia was frozen in an awkward half-crouch as she stared at this face. Dawn rapidly spread rosy tendrils of light around them all, illuminating the Odentian captain's face.

Kaia could see no compassion in his eyes.

Finnegan grabbed her arm and dragged her to her feet. He shoved her to where the rest of the witches were gathered, standing in a defensive line between the warriors and Lee.

"No more magic," Finnegan snarled, pointing his sword at each of them. "You will all submit to drink a sleeping draught and put up no more fights against us, or we will subdue you forcefully, kill whomever we need to kill to make our point clear, and take the survivors anyway."

But they had used a blunted arrow against Lee. Even though Kaia knew they had intended him harm, she still had difficulty understanding what Finnegan meant. If they hadn't killed Lee outright, how could they think to kill a bunch of teenagers? It made no sense! Her head pounded with her confusion, a throbbing that matched the beat of her heart.

"You can't mean that, though," Kaia blurted as the others crowded closer to each other.

Finnegan glared at her. "I am tiring of your back talk. I do mean it. Now shut up before I make an example out of you."

"But adults don't hurt children."

Finnegan pointed his sword at her again. But he squinted rather than snarled at her again. It was as though he didn't quite understand what she was saying. Kaia stared back.

It all had to be for show. They were trying to frighten the children into behaving to make it easier on them. That sort of violence just didn't happen. How could it? They were unarmed. Even the little bursts of magic they had used against the Odentian warriors had been flukes more than anything else.

"I don't understand," Kaia continued. Her voice was pitched with fear, but she couldn't stop herself. "Why?"

"Why what?" Finnegan demanded.

"Why are you doing this? Why do you want to hurt us?"

"Your kingdom hordes magic."

"If this is how you treat children, what else can you expect?" Kaia stepped forward. She shook her head as her shoulders slumped. "I lived at the palace this last summer. I know we offered Odentia help. Food, supplies, help to increase your crop yields—"

"Shut up."

"I just don't understand," she repeated. "If you want what's best for your kingdom, why are you here? Why aren't you at your own palace, convincing your king to accept our freely given aid?"

"I said shut up. You're a child; you can't possibly understand."

Kaia threw her hands into the air. "That's exactly what I'm saying! I don't understand. How will magic help your kingdom when your king refuses what you need to feed your people? Magic will not solve any of that. It'll only be misused and bring misery down on us all."

Finnegan stalked forward. "I told you to shut up. Don't you understand what that means?"

He pointed his sword at her again, and Kaia shrank back. Her life had never been threatened before. And even though she couldn't entirely accept that even someone like Finnegan would harm her, he still terrified her.

"She's right, though," Adina said, her voice trembling. "If you want magic for your kingdom, you need to prove that you won't misuse it. You must stop resorting to violence when there are other means of—"

"Do none of you understand what it means to be silent?" Finnegan roared. He swung around, stalking toward Adina now. "You are nobody. You are nothing. Stop babbling the nonsense you've been force-fed by your weak parents. What good is your superiority complex when I hold all your lives in my hands?"

Adina started back into his eyes, her shoulders shaking. Kaia started forward to stand with her, to offer her support, but Finnegan pointed his sword at her before she took two steps.

Kaia swallowed dryly. "Does it make you feel powerful to threaten a bunch of unarmed children?"

Finnegan stared at her. Something flashed in his eyes, but Kaia couldn't read the emotion. All she knew was that once it was gone, the fury on his face took new levels. His lip curled back as he barked out a laugh.

"Idiot children more like."

It occurred to Kaia that, though he kept speaking and though his expression was angry, the rest of the warriors were silent. They hung back, letting him take the lead. She tore her gaze from Finnegan to search the faces of the others. Some looked back without compassion; others shifted guiltily on the spot. Still, others seemed to consider her words.

"Violence is the natural order of things," Finnegan continued. "The strong consume the weak, and there is no other way. Now, are you going to shut up and submit? Or do I kill you?"

"What do you mean when you say there is no other way?" Adina demanded.

Finnegan swung around. His fist flew lightning-fast and smashed into Adina's mouth. Kaia let out a yelp as Lena and Jalene gasped. Wickham ignored Finnegan and rushed to Adina's side as she dropped to the ground. Blood dripped from her nose as she looked up at him with wide eyes.

"Why would you do that?" Kaia cried. She couldn't even make herself rush to her friend's side. "She was right! There are plenty of ways to resolve differences without violence. You say the strong crush the weak, and that's the only way? That's the exact opposite of what Eldavon does. How can you say that your way is better than ours when you're trying to steal what we have?"

"Enough!" Finnegan bellowed.

He lifted his sword and swung it at her. Time seemed to slow down. Kaia knew what was coming. It was like she could see the passage of time in her future, the steel blade coming down on her and cutting through her skin, stealing her life. And yet she still stood there, her mind unable to process it. Unable to fully believe that anyone would want to kill another person, especially like this—

"No!" Icarus cried. He pushed through Lena and Jalene and threw himself in front of Kaia.

The sword flashed. It cut across his chest. There was a tearing noise as his shirt ripped beneath the blade. Finnegan's expression didn't change, still mad with fury. Kaia caught Icarus as he stumbled back, and his cry suddenly choked off.

He did it.

Finnegan really did it.

He had been trying to kill her.

And now...

Icarus...

His weight sagged against her. Kaia held onto him tightly, but she wasn't strong enough. Her knees shook, then buckled. They went down together as blood soaked the front of Icarus' shirt. He gasped for breath, his eyes wide and skin pale.

"He-help," he whimpered.

"Wickham!" Kaia shouted. She lowered Icarus to the ground and tore off her overshirt, wadding it into the wound across his chest. Blood stained her hands as Finnegan stood motionless over them. "Wickham, help! *Please!*"

❧

WICKHAM LEFT Adina and rushed to Icarus. Finnegan let him, though Wickham half expected to feel the sword plunge through his back. The cut was shallow; that was good. It meant no vital organs had been perforated.

But the cut was long, and it was bleeding heavily. If they didn't stop the bleeding, Icarus' body would go into shock and start shutting down.

"Hold this here," he directed Kaia, trying to keep his voice from shaking.

He'd treated injuries that one person gave to another deliberately. But the worst he'd seen was a broken nose. Normally it was bruises, a few cuts maybe. The twins could get into some terrible fights when they were overly tired...

But nothing like this.

He had never seen to injuries where someone deliberately tried to kill another person!

My fault. I voted to stay put. We should have kept moving.

Wickham shook that off. No time for thinking about that sort of thing, not when there was an injury here. "I need yarrow. And, and, and—" His stammering made his tongue feel swollen. What did he need? "Water. Boiled water. Clean rags. If I can stitch the wound shut—"

"I told you someone would die if you didn't surrender," Finnegan interrupted. His voice was icy. "Now, someone will."

"We'll surrender," Kaia said. She knelt next to Icarus, gripping his hand. "We'll surrender. Please. Please, just give Wick what he needs—"

She cried out as Finnegan grabbed her hair and yanked her head back. He put his bloody sword to her throat, and Wickham's heart froze. He was already launching himself forward before he knew what he was doing—but a heavy hand clubbed him on the back of the head, knocking him over Icarus.

The warrior who had hit him dragged Wickham to a kneeling position and yanked his hands behind his back.

"No!" Adina screamed. "Don't!"

Finnegan glared over his shoulder. "Why shouldn't I?"

"Because I'm the one you were sent for. I'm the new king and queen's daughter." Adina shook like a leaf but still walked forward, her eyes never leaving Finnegan's. "I'll go with you so long as none of the others are harmed. So long as you leave them here."

Finnegan twisted his sword, scraping the edge lightly over Kaia's skin. Wickham could see her fighting back a whimper. He struggled against the hands holding him down.

"Stay still, boy," the warrior whispered in his ear, sounding gentler than Wickham could have expected. "It won't help no one to get yourself on the captain's bad side. Stand down, and your princess might still win this."

Wickham wanted to tell him that Adina wasn't a princess yet—her parents hadn't been coronated. But all his words got lost in the lump in his throat. His skin ached as though he could feel what Kaia was feeling.

Finnegan laughed harshly. "We can take you with us, anyway."

"Can you?"

Finnegan's arrogant expression froze. He started forward, only to stop. Several of the Odentian warriors made disbelieving noises.

Despite himself, Wickham tore his eyes from Kaia. He gasped.

Adina held a small dagger to her own throat. She still shook, but the determination blazed in her eyes like a fire. Wickham stared at her, his heart thudding hard into his ribs.

"Either you let everyone else go," Adina said, her voice stiff and trembling all at once, "or you lose your biggest bargaining chip. So, what will it be? Do you kill the prize you were sent to retrieve, or will you let my friends go?"

Finnegan released Kaia. He shoved her to the ground, where she hunched over, holding herself. Sobs filled the clearing.

"Adina," Icarus said, his voice barely above a whisper as he lay wounded on the ground.

Adina slowly lowered her knife, her eyes not leaving Finnegan. "You can tie me up. You can put me to sleep. But you can't keep me alive if I don't want to be. So, you will honor our agreement. Won't you?"

Finnegan laughed but nodded.

Wickham's arms were suddenly released, and he pitched forward. He caught himself and rose but stopped as Adina held her hand out to Lena and Jalene, who had been about to go to her.

"It's best this way," Adina said. She stepped forward. "Let's go, then. Your king is waiting."

CHAPTER
TWENTY

T hey found the first-year witches, finally.

But they were too late. Odentian warriors surrounded them. Lee lay motionless across the clearing. Adina bled from her nose while Wickham desperately tried to take care of Icarus' injuries. Penelope's breath left her lungs. She seemed to be frozen on the spot.

Last year, when Odentia took them all captive, she had somehow known exactly what to do. Now, though, all she could do was crouch in the bushes and think, *If I hadn't come, Row would have found them sooner.*

Herja's hand clenched onto Penelope's arm, pulling her from her thoughts.

But Row whispered to them, calm and self-assured. "Don't be afraid. This is what we're going to do. You two stay here, out of sight."

With his plumed helmet, the captain grabbed Adina's arm and turned her roughly, tying her hands behind her back.

"Once Adina is free, get in there. Get everyone moving. You're going to have to carry Lee and Icarus." Row turned Penelope, their dark silver eyes boring into hers. "If they're dead, leave them."

"I..." Penelope felt the weight of Row's instructions. Her eyes were wide with terror as she nodded slowly. "I understand."

"Herja," Row said, turning to her.

Herja straightened, her skin pale beneath her inky black hair.

"Trust your gut. Penelope will get everyone on the move, but you will lead them through the swamp. Stay off the paths." Row looked between the two girls.

If Row felt any fear, they didn't show it. Penelope wished she could be half as composed as they were. Her heart still pounded in her throat, but she nodded once more. Row knew what they were doing... and she would obey.

"Be careful," Herja whispered.

Row grinned. "Don't worry. I always am."

Penelope crouched lower as Row slid back, not disturbing the foliage. It looked as though the Odentian captain was arguing with Adina now, though quiet enough that Penelope couldn't hear what they were saying.

What would she tell Row's mate if they didn't return? For that matter, did Row have a mate? Why weren't they here...?

She shoved those thoughts aside. They weren't useful; they weren't going to help anyone.

The bushes on the other side of the clearing rustled, and Row stepped through. Though they wore no armor, only simple clothes that had gotten crusted with dirt in the swamp, they still held a powerful aura that seemed to overshadow the Odentian warriors.

"Please release Miss Adina," Row said, voice even and calm. "I don't think you want this to escalate."

The captain shoved Adina to one of his men and laughed. He pointed a sword with dried blood crusted on it at Row. "What do you think you can do? I have six men here. Do you really think that one warrior will do anything against us?"

Row cocked their head, still calm.

Penelope held her breath. Didn't the captain realize he was facing a dragon? Or was the captain so ill-informed of magic that he couldn't recognize Row's glowing silver eyes?

"I'm not a warrior," Row said simply. "I'm a professor, and these are my students. Now let Adina and the rest of them go before I become angry."

"A *professor*?" The captain looked Row up and down. "That's whom the Eldavon crown sends? A teacher? You're more pathetic than I could have possibly given you credit for! Come on, then, Professor! Show me what you got."

The captain laughed as he held his sword with both hands in front of him.

Herja let out a ragged breath. "He has no idea what he's getting himself into."

"What do you—" Penelope started, but the answer soon became clear.

Row's body seemed to shiver. A blinding light flashed out, making Penelope flinch. It was the same sort of light that came from her parents when they took their dragon form. Spots blinded her momentarily, but she gasped when the light faded.

The dragon's narrow head was sleek. Their silver eyes gleamed like small moons amid black scales that glinted with blue, green, and purple hues. Their underbelly was reddish, wings spreading out to either side bigger than any Penelope had seen before. Spikes ran down the length of their spine, a club at the end of their tail.

Penelope thought all dragons looked like her parents, siblings, the others on the Fire Watch...

She had never seen a dragon look as elegant and deadly as Professor Farrow.

Now she understood what Herja meant. There was no way this Odentian captain could stand against Row. They were saved. It was clear already. She started straightening in her hiding spot, but Herja grabbed her wrist and yanked her back down.

"Remember our orders," Herja hissed.

Penelope sank back down. Orders. Right. They needed to obey Row's orders... no matter what.

THE ODENTIAN WARRIORS closed in on Row as the captain snarled and brandished his weapon. "I've been trained to kill dragons! Your head will look good mounted on my wall, Beast!"

Herja shuddered at the horrifying proclamation. She fought to focus, to keep her eyes on where Adina was being held rather than the fight. Swords clashing. Scales scattering. Row's tail whipped out, collided with an Odentia warrior, and sent him flying—but the warrior was replaced by another in seconds.

And the captain hung back, yelling orders and not getting into the fray himself. What a coward! Herja would have liked to rush him, to knock him into the path of Row's attack—

Focus. Mission. Adina.

Herja drew in a breath, then let it out. Row was retreating in front of the warriors. They dodged forward, then pulled back, leading them away inch by inch.

"They're taking the warriors away from us," Penelope whispered. "They're sacr—"

"Don't say it," Herja snapped.

Row would get out of this. They all would. The warriors would not kill any of them. *If Lee and Icarus are dead, leave them.*

No, they won't be dead. We're going to get out of this. We're going to survive—all of us.

The last warrior, the one holding Adina, shoved her away. He drew his sword and rushed the dragon with the rest of them. It was time.

Herja and Penelope rose from the bushes and sprinted toward the other students.

Trust my gut. Stay off the paths... Brownie nest. We need a brownie nest, get them to fight for us if we're attacked again. Herja smiled. She knew just how to find them, too.

ICARUS WAS STILL BREATHING, if barely. Wickham tightened the belt he'd wrapped around the other boy's chest. He was still bleeding, but there wasn't anything Wickham could do without more resources. He had already tried a spell but couldn't reach the barest flicker of magic in himself.

"Herja?" Kaia gasped. "Penelope?"

Wickham lifted his head. At first, he was certain he must be hallucinating. How else could the two dragons be here? Then, Penelope bent over Icarus and pulled him over her shoulders.

"We have to move now. Lena, get Adina and cut her free. Wick, Kaia, and Jalene, you carry Professor Lee," Penelope ordered. She hefted Icarus up, making him groan in pain.

"Follow me," Herja said. "And we're going to be attacked by brownies. When we are, drop to the ground, stay still, and start humming."

Wickham opened his mouth to protest, but the sounds of battle were getting louder again. He dashed for Lee and lifted a corner. Herja led the way, with Adina and Lena hurrying after her, the three carrying the stretcher next, and Penelope coming up last with Icarus.

"You should have just let them take me away," Adina sobbed as she stumbled. "You should have—"

"No, we shouldn't have," Herja said over her shoulder. "Now hurry! We need to get out of sight."

KAIA WASN'T sure how long they trudged through the swamp. Branches whacked her, and bugs chomped down on her, but all she kept thinking of was how silent everything was. Herja finally called for a stop beneath the buzzing nest of a colony of brownies. The brownies came out to inspect them, but so long as the children remained low and quiet, the brownies were content to watch.

Gently, they lowered Lee to the ground. Kaia rushed over to Penelope to help her with Icarus. His head lolled as they got him to the ground.

Herja ripped open her pack and pulled out her book bag. "I've got herbs. What do you need?"

"Everything you have," Wickham replied tersely.

Kaia started gathering wood. If there was one thing she'd learned about tending to injuries, they needed lots of clean water. She gestured for Lena to help her, and soon they had enough to get a small fire going.

"We don't have our cooking pot," Jalene said.

"Don't worry," Herja replied, reaching into her book bag. "We do."

Kaia grinned at her, despite the desperation of their situation. "I knew I missed you for a reason."

Herja seemed startled at that, then smiled back. "We need more tinder for the fire. There's some dry grass over there."

Kaia nodded. She hurried over, surprised when the grass came easily. It had already been severed at the base. Looking closer, she realized it had been laid there on purpose. Brushing the grass aside, she frowned. There were silver-green objects beneath. Gems?

No... eggs...

Her heart jumped into her throat as a rattling noise sounded around them.

"Oh no..."

TWENTY-ONE

Emerald scales glittered as the gigantic snake lowered itself from the trees. Kaia remained frozen where she was. Her eyes skimmed over the barbed spikes that ran down the snake's back. They vibrated, producing that distinctive rattling noise.

Behind her, the brownies started buzzing. Her blood rushed into her ears as she remained where she was, her eyes locked with the massive animal. Golden eyes stared back as it opened its mouth, revealing fangs dripping with venom.

Run, a voice in her head yelled. *Get away from the eggs.*

Her body wouldn't obey. She was locked in her crouched position, both hands filled with the yellowed grass that covered the rattleback's nest.

Kaia, back up slowly.

That wasn't coming from her head. Kaia finally managed to pull in a breath. Someone was speaking behind her in a low voice.

"Lower your eyes and back up slowly. Kaia, listen to me!" that was Herja. Her voice was low and urgent.

Lower your eyes. Kaia dropped her head, gazing at the ground beneath her feet. The rattling grew more intense. If she could have, she would have screamed as the snake slithered closer.

"Back up slowly," Herja repeated.

Right. Kaia forced her leg to move. She slid it back, then slid the other one. With her heart in her throat, she shuffled backward as the snake drew closer. Wild thoughts raced through her mind as she tried to think of everything she knew about the Emerald Rattleback. But her mind wouldn't settle on anything.

"Look, it doesn't want to attack," Herja said softly. "Look at how it's rolling its body over the nest. It wants to protect its eggs. It's not attacking."

Kaia could hardly understand the words. Her foot met something as she shuffled backward. She froze again, imagining a second snake behind her. She let out a blood-curdling scream when something grabbed her.

The snake rose, the bristling spines along its back flaring bigger. A deep, rumbling sound filled the air. The brownies, who had been buzzing about, all fled back into their nest.

"It's okay," Penelope said. She pulled Kaia back further. "It's just me. I have you."

Shaking, Kaia grabbed onto Penelope's arm. The snake swayed back and forth, and as the children backed away, it advanced.

The bushes rustled, and Finnegan emerged. His face gleamed with sweat, that same furious look he'd had when he almost killed Kaia burning in his eyes. His armor was punctured in spots, and fire had scorched the plumes off his helmet.

"Enough of this!" he roared as he came for the students. "I'm so sick and tired of you little—"

The rattleback struck. Fangs gleaming, it sprang across the clearing. Finnegan twisted in time for the snake to ram into him. Its fangs pierced through his armor, and a scream ripped from the man. It made Kaia's blood turn cold.

Shaking its head back and forth, the Rattleback threw Finnegan; he hit a tree with a sickening crunch and dropped to the ground, unmoving.

Then, those golden eyes turned back to the students.

PENELOPE GRABBED the nearest branch and smashed it as hard as she could against a tree. The Emerald Rattleback, which had been slithering all the closer to the other students, swung its head around. Penelope waved the stick and banged it against the tree again.

In the swamp's silence, her shouting seemed impossibly loud. If she could distract the snake, get it away from the others long enough for them to escape—

As it lunged for her, though, Penelope suddenly realized what a mistake she had made. With the brownies, they didn't stop attacking the three dragons until after they'd proven themselves not to be a threat. Being loud and disruptive, she only pushed the rattleback into thinking they were all threats. She should have been quiet. Should have—

A roar blasted in her ears as something slammed into her. She gasped, expecting the stabbing pain of fangs piercing through her body at any second... a scream built in her throat.

She hit the ground, driving the air from her lungs, and curled into a ball. Adrenaline spiked through her body as she waited for the pain to set in. Something wrapped around her, and she lashed out, trying to fight off the snake—only to realize that it wasn't the thick, sinuous body of a snake but multiple sets of hands.

Row was in the center of the clearing, and wings spread wide to either side as they faced off with the Emerald Rattleback. The rattling met with a low growl as the two wove back and forth, each looking for a place to strike....

Or were they waiting for the other to strike?

Penelope looked around quickly. The other students were in a tight-knit ball around Lee on the stretcher, but the Rattleback had left its nest in the chaos. Its attention was fully locked on Row as it drew itself up, hissing.

"Penelope," Herja whispered. "Come on! We have to get out of here."

"Wait," Penelope's mind raced.

The snake hadn't become aggressive toward them until after the Odentian warrior arrived, and she had banged on that tree. Even now, it wasn't attacking Row, though it seemed like the tension would snap at any moment.

Would it work? If the snake wanted them away from its nest, they couldn't leave without leaving Row...

"Get Professor Lee off the stretcher," she said, moving backward to join the other students.

"What? No, we have to—"

Penelope turned to Herja, even though turning her back on the potential fight felt wrong. "Move Lee off the stretcher. We're going to move the Rattleback's eggs onto the stretcher, so it can take them away... it'll be easier for the snake to leave than us. It moves out. We stay here."

Herja opened her mouth, then paused. With a desperate glance at Row, she nodded once. "That might just work... or it will cause the snake to attack, seeing us messing with its nest."

"I know. Now let's get Lee off the stretcher. We have to move quickly."

HOW WAS this supposed to work? Wickham's hands shook as he carefully lifted one of the emerald eggs and put it on the stretcher. His thoughts were in a loop, telling him this was wrong, this was dangerous.

They should have just taken Lee and left. Once they were gone, Professor Farrow could leave the Rattleback, and they'd all be fine....

But they didn't have a stretcher for Icarus. They couldn't move him and didn't know the extent of the damage he had suffered. And

Finnegan's body was still slumped beneath the tree. Was he alive or dead? There was no way of knowing if they just left.

They couldn't escape unless they left at least two injured people behind. Wickham couldn't bring himself to consider leaving behind the Odentian leader, no matter what he'd done.

And Penelope spoke with so much authority, Wickham couldn't find it in himself to argue with her. He just hoped that they hadn't made a mistake, that she knew what she was doing. Because if she didn't, they were all doomed.

Wickham pushed those thoughts aside as he moved faster. He and Herja moved the eggs onto the stretcher while Lena and Jalene packed the dry grass around them. Penelope stood guard, watching the standoff between Professor Farrow and the Emerald Rattleback.

"Careful," Herja hissed at him as two eggs clinked together.

Wickham wasn't listening, though. He'd turned, hearing a soft, gasping noise from Icarus. Blood was bubbling at his lips, and Wickham dove away, accidentally kicking Herja as he made his way to Icarus' side. He pivoted Icarus to his side, his stomach squeezing with panic as blood trailed from the other student's mouth.

"I need help," he called—only to remember too late.

The snake heard his call, and its attention was directed from Professor Farrow just long enough to see what the students were doing. It let out an enraged roar that sounded almost dragon-like and lunged for them. Professor Farrow struck, shielding the students with their wings.

Wickham couldn't see what happened next; he could only hear the vicious, snarling noises that made the hairs on the back of his neck stand on end.

Despite the noise and confusion, he focused on Icarus. The bleeding had almost stopped from his chest, but this new bleeding from his mouth showed something had been punctured internally. His breathing was ragged. But once Wickham turned him on his side to help the blood drain out, it became easier.

But what was happening? Icarus had shown no signs of internal bleeding before. Wickham had no more herbs to use in a spell; he had little energy left.

What should he do?

What *could* he do?

Focus on keeping him breathing. Wickham stabilized Icarus' head, keeping him in a position where the blood wouldn't flow back into his throat. Then, he realized it wasn't coming from his mouth, at least not primarily—it was his nose. What gave him a nosebleed?

Wickham felt Icarus' forehead. He was feverish.

Poison. It had to be. Finnegan must have poisoned his blade. A chill swept through Wickham. *Why?*

THE LAST OF the eggs were on the stretcher. Herja grabbed the bottom, and Penelope grabbed the top, lifting it up.

"Go to Lee and Wickham," Penelope ordered Lena and Jalene tensely. Her eyes were locked on the battle.

Herja's heart thumped in her chest. "What's the plan, then?"

"We show the snake it can take its eggs away from us and... hope," Penelope replied.

Herja opened her mouth to argue but swallowed—no point in arguing now. The sounds of the fight were growing more dreadful. To Herja's horror, Row's wings were shrinking. The glitter of their scales disappeared, and they seemed to contract, writhing in pain.

They dropped to the ground, panting, in natural form once more. The snake loomed over them; then its head snapped around to Herja and Penelope.

"Stay calm," Penelope said.

Herja would have replied that it was impossible, but her throat was utterly dry. She'd never seen a creature as giant as this, let alone with its hostile attention on her. She trembled, fighting to keep a firm grip on the rough branches of the stretcher.

Penelope let out a shaky breath. "Follow my lead."

Together, they approached the Rattleback. Herja's heart froze as the spikes along its back shivered together, but she kept her eyes down, trying not to appear threatening. They moved slowly and turned slightly to show the eggs to the snake.

Its hissing died away as it lowered itself back down. Penelope set her side down, and Herja hastily followed suit; they moved too quickly, and the rattling started back up. But when they froze, the snake went silent. It watched them as though it was working out exactly what they were doing.

"All right, let's put it down gently," Penelope whispered.

Together, they lowered the stretcher to the ground. Herja stayed bent, but Penelope straightened.

"No, stay low," Herja quickly told her. "Rattlebacks only lift themselves as a threat display. Stay low, and we signal we're not threatening."

Penelope let out a surprised sound but bent again. She reached for Herja's arm and tugged her back away from the nest toward Row. They were still on the ground, panting and wheezing.

"Help me with them," Penelope said as she reached for Row's arms.

The snake hissed at them again. Herja tugged Penelope to her knees, following suit herself. They knelt with their heads toward the ground, positioned between the snake and Row. The snake lifted its head, its tongue flicking out and back in several times.

"It's tasting the air," Herja whispered. She wasn't sure why she said it, only that there was this weird compulsion as if by explaining the snake's behavior, she could make it do what they wanted. "It's how they smell. So, it's smelling everything around us."

The Rattleback lowered its head and nudged the eggs on the stretcher. Herja held her breath. *Please be right. Please just take them and go....*

TWENTY-TWO

Penelope could hardly hold in the scream building in her throat. The Emerald Rattleback coiled itself around the stretcher with the eggs, lifting it gingerly. Its movements were careful, catching the stretcher through the fabric on both sides. Then it slithered off into the swamp, its movements jerky as it kept the stretcher stable.

Once it was out of sight, Penelope finally allowed herself to drop to the ground. She rolled to her back, sucking in deep breaths as the emotions of everything that happened washed through her. She shook so badly that she didn't have the strength to hold herself up.

It worked. The Rattleback was gone. They were safe... for now, at least.

"What's wrong with Professor Farrow?" Lena asked.

Penelope lifted her head. The danger of the Rattleback had passed, but they still had work to do.

"The venom from an Emerald Rattleback suppresses the dragon," Herja replied. "It will knock Row out for a few hours, but they'll be fine."

"Row?" Wickham repeated. He had moved away from Icarus and Professor Lee to clean up Row's injuries.

Penelope pulled herself into a sitting position. "That's what they told us to call them while we were in the swamp. We keep using it because that was the last thing we were told."

Wickham nodded. "Lee told us just to use his name, too."

"Good to know," Penelope murmured. She got to her feet, brushing herself off as she took stock of the situation. Three were down with injuries and an enemy soldier whose status was unknown. That was the first thing they needed to establish. "Herja, help me with the Odentian warrior."

"Finnegan," Lena said. She still knelt beside Wickham and Row.

Adina and Jalene were back with Icarus and Lee. Adina sobbed into Jalene's shoulder, both leaning into a tree as though they no longer had the strength to do anything else.

"Kaia," Penelope called. "Take Jalene and Adina to gather wood; we need a fire to keep warm. If you can collect any sort of food, that would be good. Water is more important, though."

Kaia stepped toward the other two witches, her face pale. She opened her mouth, then closed it again.

The three didn't speak as they got up and obeyed Penelope's orders.

Would they be all right out in the swamp? Was it dangerous to send them off?

Penelope pushed thoughts of them aside for the moment. One thing at a time. They needed warmth, water, and food. Herja's bag only gave them so much. Besides, they were going to need some place for their enemy.

She and Herja moved to Finnegan and checked his pulse; his heart was beating, his eyes were shut, his skin pale. A trickle of drool ran down his chin.

"Let's get his armor off him, search him for weapons, and tie him up," Penelope said.

Herja nodded once.

"Careful when dealing with his weapons," Wickham called. "I think they're poisoned."

Penelope nodded. It made sense. If Odentia knew that Rattleback's venom could suppress the dragon, they would have wanted to use it against all the dragons they encountered.

They carefully straightened the Odentian warrior out, then started unbuckling his armor. The leather connections had been charred in places, and the girls were forced to cut through those bindings to remove the armor.

Penelope found two knives in short order, one at his hip, the other in his boot. Herja removed the boots entirely, finding a third in a secret compartment in the sole, then another two in the warrior's shirt.

Once satisfied that there were no further weapons on the man, Penelope and Herja retrieved vines from the forest and stripped them down with the knives until they were thin and malleable. They bound him tightly, then moved over to Wickham. He had packed the fang wounds on Row's body.

"You'll have to look at the Odentian man, too," Penelope told him.

Kaia, Adina, and Jalene had started a fire by this time. They worked well together, which made sense—they'd probably become very used to the routine over the last while. Wickham and Lena had gone through Herja's bag, and laid out all their supplies.

"Why do we care about him?" Jalene asked viciously, glaring at Finnegan. "He threatened to kill us and tried to kill Kaia. He's the reason Icarus is in his current state."

Penelope fought back the surge of anger at these words. "Regardless, we can't just let him suffer and die. That's not the sort of people we are."

Jalene lowered her head. None of them looked pleased with the situation, but Wickham moved to Finnegan and treated his injuries.

"What do you need?" Penelope asked him, crouching nearby.

"His armor seems to have protected him from the worst of the injuries. Minor bleeding; head injury, though. Swelling, brain bleed... he was bitten, he'll have the venom, too." Wickham pressed his forearm across his eyes. "I need... I need herbs. I need to make a healing spell."

"What herbs?" Penelope pressed.

Wickham listed off a dozen or so. Penelope divided them among the others and sent them off, staying behind herself to monitor the camp here. She tended the fire and helped Wickham as he worked. He'd pulled together some spells that Penelope didn't understand, even though he tried to explain. The spells seemed to help Icarus' new bleeding.

"How is Row's pulse?" Wickham called over his shoulder from where he dripped a smelly spell into Lee's mouth.

Penelope checked Row's wrist and neck. Their pulse was steady, matched evenly between both points. "It's good."

"Good, good," Wickham said. "Come here and help with this, okay? Dip the cloth into the water and drip it into Lee's mouth a little at a time. Not too much, or he could drown in it."

"Drown? In a few drops?"

Wickham nodded grimly. "You'd be surprised."

"All right," Penelope nodded. She took up a position next to Wickham and took over.

Wickham thanked her and moved off again. "Where are they with those herbs?"

THE OTHERS RETURNED ALMOST at dusk. By then, Wickham was certain he had stabilized all his patients.

His patients.

He didn't dare dwell on that, knowing if he spent too much time thinking he'd easily end up overwhelmed. Best to just focus on what he knew he could do. And that was to make sure these wounds were no longer seeping, that no infection had set in, and that they were all resting comfortably so they wouldn't choke on their own vomit.

There was precious little more that he had the knowledge to do. But sitting idly by only increased his anxiety. So Wickham stayed busy, whether mixing herbs or making notes about his patients' conditions.

Eventually, Kaia brought him a bowl of weed stew. "You need to eat."

"I'd rather not," Wickham said, wrinkling his nose at the grey-green mush.

"I don't care if you'd rather not. You need to eat. How are you supposed to care for them if you get sick from starvation?" Kaia snapped.

Wickham's eyes widened as he stared at his friend in shock. He had never heard Kaia speak that way to anyone! Her eyes narrowed, her cheeks slightly flushed. He took the stew silently and bent over it, eating.

Kaia huffed and strode to the fire, where she promptly laid down a little way from the others and rolled to her side. She crunched up into a ball, her head pillowed on her arms.

She must be under a lot of stress. Wickham started to stand, to go talk with her, but a groan made him turn. Icarus was stirring, and Wickham hurriedly put his food aside and raced to his patient.

"Icarus?"

"Hurts..." Icarus whimpered.

Pain medication! What did he have for pain medication? As the others gathered, Wickham sorted through his things again. He had to have something, right?

"Adina?" Icarus called.

Adina knelt beside him and took his hand in hers. "I'm here. Wickham's looking for something to help with the pain. You're going to be fine."

Wickham was grateful that she was showing concern—it would be good for Icarus. Hopefully, it would be enough to distract him while Wickham searched for anything to help with the pain. He was out of willow bark, which wouldn't be strong enough anyway. Maybe golden fox-feather? He might have some seeds that he could grind....

"I'm sorry," Icarus said, his voice so low Wickham could hardly hear him. "I'm sorry for everything. Please forgive me... I didn't understand... I thought—"

"Shhh," Adina soothed, patting his shoulder. "It's all right. Kaia would be dead if it weren't for you. You're going to be okay. Wickham's looking after you, and we'll get back to the Institute before you know it."

Wickham finally found a few precious seeds in the bundle of herbs that the others had collected. He had dismissed them before because he focused on managing the bleeding and countering the Rattleback venom.

Now, he crushed the seeds into a little water, making a thick paste. He returned to Icarus and carefully spread the mixture under Icarus' tongue.

Icarus groaned. "Tastes bad..."

"I know, but hopefully, it will help with the pain," Wickham said. "If nothing else, it will help you sleep."

Icarus groaned again but didn't reply. Either his pain overtook him, or the seeds did their work because he was soon unconscious again. Adina remained sitting near him, worry in her eyes.

"We just have to hold on until Row wakes up," Wickham murmured, resting a hand on her shoulder. "They'll know what to do. They'll be able to get us all out of here. Everything is going to be okay."

"Do you really think so, boy?" Finnegan said.

Wickham jumped. He wasn't the only one. Lena and Jalene both uttered startled cries while Penelope and Herja rolled to their feet and quickly put themselves between the group and the Odentian leader. Kaia hurriedly joined Adina and Wickham; her hands clenched into fists.

Finnegan rolled into a sitting position with ease. At first, Wickham thought he had a remarkably swift recovery until he realized the warrior must have been pretending to be unconscious for some time as he regained his strength.

How much of their discussions had he heard? Wickham's gaze dropped to the binding on his wrists; it looked still intact. If Finnegan could have freed himself, he would have, right?

"Looks like you're in a bit of a predicament," Finnegan drawled, grinning at them all. "My warriors will find us soon. How well do you think you'll defend against them, huh? Especially with your big dragon protector out?"

Wickham's skin crawled, but Penelope folded her arms and tossed her red hair over her shoulder. "There are others from the Institute here looking for us. They'll find us soon enough."

Finnegan only smiled at her. "If that was the case, why haven't they found you already? The sounds from the swamp—"

"Wouldn't have traveled," Herja interrupted.

Finnegan looked at her. "Oh?"

"Dragons and humans can't hear long distances in the Silent Marshes. Hence they're called *silent,*" Herja said. She cocked her head and narrowed her eyes at him. "But I think you knew that already, didn't you? An Odentian captain, you would have had plenty of learning before they sent you here. Especially since you got into the heart of Eldavon without being detected."

"Aren't you a clever girl?" Finnegan said, narrowing his eyes.

"Clever enough for my age and how much experience I've had, although I haven't dealt with spies before." Herja turned to Penelope. "We shouldn't engage with him. We don't know what he's after, and we could easily give away more information than we realize."

Penelope nodded and picked up Finnegan's sword. His expression faltered as she pointed it at him. "Get the bag, Herja. We're putting this spy away."

TWENTY-THREE

innegan straightened, looking alarmed. "You don't have the guts! You Eldavon are against violence."

Herja straightened her book bag and frowned as she returned to stand at Penelope's side. What was he talking about? Nobody said anything about violence. Herja resisted the urge to demand answers. For all she knew, this could just be another trick to make them give up something. Penelope had already accidentally given away that while there were others in the swamp, the students had no way to contact them.

And I confirmed that they would not come to our rescue if we screamed enough, Herja realized.

Finnegan glared at the two of them. "If you kill me—"

"Who said anything about killing you?" Kaia said.

"You, shut up! I've had enough of your smart mouth," Finnegan snapped at her.

Penelope, Herja, and Adina all growled together. Penelope started forward but stopped as she glanced at the sword. Snorting, she lowered the blade toward the ground. Ah, she understood what this was about, then. Good. Herja didn't.

"If you think you're going to lure me in close enough so you can steal this back from me, you're mistaken," she said, her voice calm.

Right. Yes, Penelope might be strong, but Finnegan was clearly stronger, not to mention trained. If Penelope got too close, it would no doubt be easy for Finnegan to take the weapon back from her. So how were they going to get him into the bag?

She nodded toward Herja. "Is the bag ready?"

Herja laid it on the ground, propping the opening wide with a few sticks. "Go ahead and get inside," she said.

Finnegan stared at the bag. "What?"

"Get in," Penelope repeated. "You are our prisoner."

She sounded somewhat smug about it, too. Herja couldn't help but smile. She had thought Penelope was a straight arrow, unwilling to break the rules. And yet, here she was. First sneaking them into the search party and now putting this Odentian warrior in his place.

"What's in it?" Finnegan demanded.

"A self-cleaning chamber pot and a few water skins to keep you alive until we're back at the Institute," Herja replied, propping her hands against her hips. The chamber pot had been a lucky find when they risked leaving their hiding place to use the toilet one night.

A lucky find but also a lifesaver.

"No scorpions?" Finnegan asked. "No bed of nails?"

Herja scoffed. "If we don't have the guts to kill you, what makes you think we'd be comfortable torturing you?"

A low groan made her turn. Row pushed themselves to a seated position, rubbing their head. "It's a good idea, girls. Just wait a moment."

Relief washed over Herja. A lump swelled in her throat, and she nearly bounded across the clearing to throw her arms around the professor. Wickham called out in relief as he hurried to Row's side while Lena, Jalene, Adina, and Kaia rushed over. Kaia twisted her hands, looking like she was about to cry.

Finnegan inched toward Penelope, who had half-turned to Row, but he stopped when Herja threw a clump of dirt at him.

Row stood, reassuring the witches gently, before checking on Lee

154

and Icarus. Wickham spoke quietly, too quiet for Herja to hear, and Row nodded every so often. Once Wickham was done, Row put a hand on his shoulder.

"You've done a good job, Wickham. Have you been taking care of yourself as well?" Row asked, their back not quite turned to Finnegan.

Herja had a feeling the Professor was monitoring him, even while checking on the students.

Wickham picked up a bowl from the ground and ate.

Then, Row turned to Finnegan. Their expression was blank as they strode forward, studying their prisoner. Finnegan stuck his chin out and sneered with an arrogant look that made Herja want to say or do something to make him show respect.

"Now that you aren't trying to kill me, why don't you tell me your name?" Row asked, crouching to be at eye level with Finnegan.

"I am Captain Finnegan of his Majesty's forces. And you would be best served by untying me before my warriors destroy you all," Finnegan replied.

Row tilted their head to one side. "Captain? That's an impressive rank for someone so young. You can't be over nineteen, can you?"

Herja's nose wrinkled. She'd always been bad at guessing ages, but as she studied Finnegan, she didn't think he looked that young. He was an adult for sure, with his muscular frame and the stubble growing on his chin and around his mouth.

"I'm a captain. My age is irrelevant," Finnegan insisted, though his cheeks colored.

Row hummed, then stood.

"You should untie me anyway," the prisoner continued. "You can't fly them all out here. And if you kill me, my warriors will wreak havoc on your kingdom. My king will make Eldavon suffer heavily for my death."

Herja glanced over everyone, and her heart sank. It was true. They couldn't all fly out. Especially not when Lee and Icarus both desperately needed medical care. Row didn't seem to be paying attention to Finnegan's words anymore, though. Their face was turned upward toward the sky.

Night had fallen, bringing with it an almost restful dark. Herja wished she could allow it to lull her to sleep. She was exhausted.

"Let me check the bag," Row said abruptly.

They wormed their way into the bag, and Herja was amused to see Finnegan's eyes bug out at the sight. After a few minutes, Row reappeared, bringing a handful of items the students had left behind. Then, they searched Finnegan—finding two more knives that Herja and Penelope had missed—and sent the prisoner inside.

"You'll have to keep him in there," Row said as they tied the top of the bag shut. "He has enough food and water to last three days, so you don't have to worry about that. Don't let him out for anything, understood?"

Herja wrapped her arms around her middle. "Why does it sound like you're leaving?"

"Because they have to," Penelope said. She dropped Finnegan's sword and rubbed her temples.

Herja already knew that was the answer, the only answer. They were too far from help to get out of here on their own, not with their injured in their current states. If they tried to make it out on foot, Icarus and Lee would undoubtedly die.

Knowing Row had to leave to save Icarus and Lee didn't make it any easier for Herja to process their departure. She thought she was used to being on her own, but nobody had left her before... not like this, at least.

She was always the one who left.

I'm not alone, though, she thought as she glanced at Penelope. *And just like Row, I know what I need to do.*

"We'll take care of the witches," Herja said, forcing herself to straighten.

A wrinkle formed between Row's eyebrows as their gaze shifted around the group. They seemed to hesitate a moment before they nodded. "Look after each other, all of you."

"We will," Penelope promised.

Row got to work preparing two slings to carry Lee and Icarus. Herja found a few large stones to pin over the top of her book bag, ensuring

Finnegan couldn't escape. Then, she set about organizing their supplies a little better.

"Wait here until I return," Row said once they were ready. "I'm going to take Lee and Icarus to the search party's camp, and then I'll come back for the rest of you. Use branches and thorn bushes to build yourself a fence around the clearing, but don't go too far. I'll be back soon."

⚜

PENELOPE WATCHED Row disappear into the dark sky. A weight settled over her. She hated the idea of sitting here waiting for their rescue to come. What if Finnegan was right, and his warriors attacked them? What if he got free?

"We shouldn't try to do anything more tonight," Herja murmured, appearing suddenly at her side.

Penelope jumped. She turned to everyone watching the two dragons with anxious expressions.

"I..." Her throat was dry, so Penelope swallowed and straightened herself. They were all looking to her for reassurance now that Row was gone. "We should all get some sleep. Tomorrow, we'll organize ourselves into search parties, and start fortifying our position. We'll also review our supplies and determine how much we need to ration. With any luck, we won't need to eat more weed stew."

This elicited a few chuckles, and Penelope felt herself straighten further. Chuckling meant everyone felt a little better, right?

She hoped it did, at least.

"I'll take first watch," Adina volunteered. She looked at the others, and her gaze lingered on Kaia before moving to Lena. "Will you watch with me?"

"Sure," Lena agreed.

Penelope nodded. "Make sure you keep an eye on the book bag, too. If there's any sign Finnegan is getting out, wake us up."

"Sure," Adina murmured.

Penelope found her bedding and stretched out, suddenly utterly exhausted. Tomorrow would be a new day... and hopefully the last they would spend out here.

PENELOPE WOKE everyone up early the next morning, just as dawn was peering through the foliage. The students made a tally of their supplies, then took some time to discuss their current situation. It was decided that they would ration everything for three days, the same amount of time that Finnegan had food and water for.

After that, the adults should have found them again.

Once that was decided, Penelope arranged everyone into three groups. Adina and Lena would stay at camp and sleep. Jalene would keep watch and wake them if there were any signs of danger. Wickham and Herja would go together to look for herbs and gather firewood, while she and Kaia would collect firewood, larger branches, and thorny bushes to build a wall around their camp.

Kaia was oddly quiet as she and Penelope ventured into the swamp. The dark circles under her blue eyes spoke to a sleepless night, but Penelope thought it seemed more than that.

"Are you okay?" Penelope asked after some time.

Kaia nodded. "I'm fine."

Well, that certainly sounded like a lie. Penelope frowned as she lowered her end of the massive fallen tree they had found—it would be a good prop to weave the thorn bushes through. Kaia was panting and sat on her end of the tree, holding her head in her hands.

"You're not fine," Penelope said.

"Yes, I am."

"Kaia, something is clearly bothering you," Penelope said as she came over to her friend. She sat next to her. "Tell me about it."

Kaia chewed her lip, and when she looked up, her eyes swam with tears. "Icarus."

"What about him?"

"He... he jumped in front of the sword. Finnegan was going to kill me, and Icarus jumped in front of the sword. I kept talking even though Finnegan told me not to. I didn't think he would really hurt me, but he was going to kill me, and then Icarus...." Kaia's shoulders hunched inward, and she hid her face again.

Penelope put an arm around her friend. "It's not your fault that Icarus got hurt."

"I should have just stopped talking. I shouldn't have—"

"Kaia, you didn't know. You said yourself you didn't think he'd hurt you." Penelope rested her chin atop Kaia's head. "We can't let ourselves get caught up in what we did. Row took Icarus away now, and it's out of our hands. We have to take care of what we have access to right now."

Kaia sniffled, leaning into Penelope. It made Penelope feel uncomfortable, but she wasn't sure why. Penelope had often comforted others in the Fire Watch. Why was Kaia so different?

It must be because I'm so used to her doing the comforting, Penelope thought.

"Let's get back to camp now," she said, patting Kaia's back. "We have a lot of work ahead of us still."

CHAPTER
TWENTY-FOUR

Wickham rested his chin in his hand, staring at the barrels that had slowly emptied over the last three days. Yesterday, they had stretched out their food for an extra day. But even so, Row and the other dragons should be back by now.

So what happened? Did the Odentian warriors find them? Was Row having a difficult time finding the other search party? Did they lose track of where the students were camped?

He closed his eyes as Lena and Adina squabbled over clearing up after supper. It was a pointless argument, and soon Kaia would step in to stop them, but these petty fights were getting increasingly common. As much relief as they'd gotten when Row first came, the tension had seeped back in.

"Will you quit yelling at each other?" Kaia snapped.

Wickham watched her as she stormed over to Adina and Lena. He thought about joining her, giving her his support. But he was on watch last night and was so tired that he didn't think he could talk to anyone without biting someone's head off.

"She refuses to do her fair share," Lena accused, pointing at Adina.

Kaia put her hands on her hips. "Her fair share was cooking breakfast and preparing enough water to clean up afterward; I see the washing basin is full, and you haven't even started. So tell me, what is Adina's fair share?"

"I'm tired," Lena whined. "And yesterday, when Adina was tired, I did her cleanup."

Adina huffed. "You volunteered to do it."

"And I'm tired today!"

Kaia stepped between them. "We're all tired, Lena. So just—"

Jalene screamed.

Wickham jerked and twisted to see a warrior wearing Odentian armor standing just inside the small opening they'd built into their ring of protection. A confused look passed over the warrior's face as he looked over the camp.

A shout came from where Penelope and Herja had been fixing more thorns into a bare section of the wall.

"Get out of here!" Penelope shouted, waving her arms over her head. "We don't want you here! Leave us alone!"

All the students scrambled to their feet, and the warrior turned around. They disappeared the way they had come. Penelope rushed over and grabbed the thorny door carefully, putting it into place.

She whirled around, her knotted red hair swishing around her. "Who was the last to leave? Who left the door open?"

Silence.

"I asked a question," Penelope demanded, advancing on the group of witches.

Wickham covered his eyes with his hands, shaking with adrenaline and exhaustion. "What does it matter? You're going to yell at whoever did it, so of course they will not tell you. That warrior is going to get the others—so what are we going to do?"

"Get everything together," Penelope said. "We're leaving—"

"No," Adina argued.

"I said—"

Adina stepped in front of Penelope, narrowing her eyes. "You said, but we haven't agreed. Professor Farrow told us to wait here."

"But they've been gone so long," Kaia said, twisting her hands.

"We were still told to wait," Adina insisted.

Despite their argument moments earlier, Lena nodded along with her. Wickham pressed his palms to his eyes. He would not get any sleep now, no matter what.

"We have the wall," Adina continued.

"Which won't do anything against their swords," Penelope argued.

"Then you should have kept Finnegan's rather than throwing it away—"

Kaia held up her hands. "Fighting will not help—we need a council."

Penelope started to argue, but Herja stepped beside Kaia and nodded. "Kaia's right. We have different options to consider here and need to discuss them as rationally as possible. We're low on supplies, our location has been discovered, and Finnegan will be out of food and water today, too."

Finnegan.

Wickham had almost forgotten all about him.

Penelope closed her eyes but nodded. Everyone gathered around the firepit, though Wickham kept shooting anxious looks toward the door. They had counted on the swamp's sound-dampening effects to keep them secret, thinking that their wall was thick enough that the Odentian warriors wouldn't be able to see through it...

Everything seemed to be falling apart now, though.

"First off, Finnegan," Herja said. "We need to know what to do with him. We can't just starve him."

Wickham's gaze moved to the crates and barrels of food they had left. Enough to feed six people for one more day. For one person, it would be enough for five or six days. Finnegan would eat more than any students here, but how much more?

"We can swap out his water skins every three days without a problem," Herja was saying while Wickham did the math in his mind. "But I don't feel comfortable opening up the bag every single day to give him new food."

"So, are you suggesting we just let him go?" Adina demanded.

Herja frowned at her. "Of course not. That would be stupid. I'm just saying, we are going to have to feed him."

"We can give him the rest of our supplies," Wickham said. He stared into the dying coals of the fire—it was a hot day out, and they hadn't wanted to keep a fire going. "The jerky, the preserves... It should be enough to last him for another five days on the inside. With any luck, he has rationed the food he has in there, too, and has some left over. We won't know until we open it up."

Adina looked over her shoulder at the supplies.

Penelope nodded her approval of Wickham's plan. "That's a good idea. We can also offer whatever fresh food we can gather as we prepare to swap out his water to help it stretch farther. We'll have to rely on Wickham's herbs to make the weed stew palatable."

Wickham sighed unhappily. Even though it was his idea, he hated the idea of eating those weeds every single meal. "I guess we don't really have a choice, do we?"

"Not a good one, at least," Jalene said.

Kaia managed a rough-looking smile at everyone. "At least we're all getting practiced at foraging, right? With any luck, we'll be able to find eggs or maybe some fish."

"A vote, then," Adina said. "Who thinks we should give Finnegan the last of our supplies?"

Wickham raised his hand. Everyone else did as well. Good. Having this one thing they all agreed on would help with the arguments the next discussion would elicit. Although he had a feeling that it was already decided, too. As much as he wanted to stay here, to wait for Professor Farrow and the other adults to show up....

They weren't here.

And the Odentian warriors were.

"Now, to the vote on what we should do now that our location has been compromised," Herja started.

"We should stay," Adina said at once. "What was the point of building this wall if we're just going to abandon it at the first sign of trouble?"

"But it's not the first sign of trouble," Penelope protested.

Adina wrinkled her nose.

Penelope didn't blink. "The first sign of trouble was that it's been three days, and the adults haven't returned. The second sign of trouble is the disturbances you and Jalene saw in the water when you went to fill the pot this morning. The third—"

"All right, I get it," Adina interrupted. "I still think we should stay. So let's vote on it, shall we?"

KAIA DIDN'T WANT to vote. She didn't want any of this to be happening. Not like she had any choice. Though she believed in the power of positivity, it was getting harder to be positive. All she could think was of were these few weeks spent running constantly, achy, tired, and always afraid.

I can't do this anymore. I can't. The Silver Springs made an awful choice. I shouldn't be a witch, I'm not strong enough.

Tears burned against her eyes. She had never once doubted her place before now. But if she weren't a witch, she wouldn't be here right now. Why didn't the Springs somehow look into her and see she wasn't strong enough to withstand something like this?

"I'm not ready to vote yet," Penelope said. "I have something more to say."

Adina huffed, making Kaia want to snap at her. This was hard enough without Adina acting like everyone was out to get her.

"I'm convinced that going deeper into the swamp is our best course of action," Penelope said. She met the gaze of each witch. "It'll be harder for the spies to find us when we're moving. And since you can hear them coming and they can't hear us, we'll be able to scatter and regroup easier. If we stay, we'll have to go out to forage, anyway. The walls won't be very useful then."

"And what about Professor Farrow?" Herja asked her tone calm.

"They will be able to find us. They know the swamp."

Herja nodded. "I agree. I believe our best chance will be to leave this place and go on the move again. However, I disagree that going deeper into the swamp is our best idea. At this point, we should try to find our way to the western border. With any luck, we'll start hitting some of the Swamp Watch's outposts."

Penelope frowned.

Don't start fighting, Kaia begged silently.

"We can decide exactly where to head once we have the vote," Penelope allowed. "Now. Who votes to stay here?"

Adina, Lena, and Jalene all lifted their hands.

Penelope smiled.

"Who votes to leave?" Adina asked, growling.

Wickham, Herja, and Penelope raised their hands.

Everyone turned to Kaia. She refused to look at any of them, digging her hands into her hair. She had a feeling that this was how it would end up. Even though Adina and Lena had been snarling and fighting lately, Jalene and Lena followed Adina's lead in these things.

"You can't just say you won't vote," Adina said.

Kaia shook her head. "I didn't say I won't vote. I haven't made up my mind."

"We have to move," Penelope urged.

"Don't push me," Kaia snapped. She lifted her head and glared at them all. "You never even bothered to ask if everyone was ready for the vote before you went ahead and called for it. So, what am I supposed to do when I can't think?"

Herja opened her mouth and closed it again.

The weight of all six of the others' eyes on her made Kaia scramble to her feet. She paced away, her head turning so she could keep an eye on the door. They both had good points. Her three closest friends were voting one way.

But they had already put so much effort into building the wall. This was where Professor Farrow told them to stay. The Odentian warriors would be able to track them as much as the dragons of Eldavon.

"I can't," she finally whispered. "I can't go running through that swamp again, not knowing where to turn, not knowing when they'll find us. At least if we're here, we can keep a fire going; we can use the barrels and crates. We can have shelter if it starts raining."

Kaia turned, looking back to the group. "I vote we stay. I'm just too tired to go back to traveling day after day while living in that fear. I'm too tired to deal with everyone arguing with each other all the time. I can't do that. So, I vote we stay."

Penelope's eyes never left her, but the other girl didn't respond to Kaia's words. "Adina, you and I will start getting everything ready to swap over with Finnegan, then. The rest of you take the barrels and crates out to gather as much fresh water and food as you can. We'll have to limit our daily foraging."

"Pen," Kaia protested.

"Go on," Penelope said. She scrambled to her feet and turned her back. "We don't have a lot of time."

No, they didn't. But it seemed like things were going to get worse around here, even if Odentia never attacked them.

Where was Professor Farrow? Kaia's heart clenched. *And why haven't my parents come looking for us, too?*

CHAPTER
TWENTY-FIVE

Since Penelope and Adina had given Finnegan the rest of the food and a barrel of fresh water, plenty to last six days, there wasn't much to do other than boil water to fill up their spare barrels.

The tension was thick between them. After the fight from earlier in the day, Penelope didn't want to risk striking it back up.

"Penelope?" Adina said after the first pot was boiling.

"Yes, Adina?"

"I just wanted to thank you for accepting the results of the vote," Adina said hesitantly. "I was certain Kaia would vote for you, since you're her friend."

Penelope frowned at Adina as she added more wood to the fire. "She didn't vote for me, though. She voted to stay. It's not personal."

Adina picked a leaf from her silvery hair. "I guess it felt personal. Like you were saying, I was being stupid for wanting to stay....."

"I didn't mean to give that impression." Penelope's frown deepened. What had she done to make Adina think that? "I'm sorry. I was only thinking about what I thought was best, just like staying is what you thought was best—and I know you have good reasons, too, so I can't be angry with you for it."

"My parents tell me I have a bad habit of jumping to conclusions," Adina admitted.

Penelope shrugged. She didn't know Adina well enough to make any sort of comment to that. And she wasn't sure why they were having this discussion at all, if she was honest. Yes, there was tension between them, but sometimes people just had tension. Penelope would rather ignore it and just continue working.

"I'm glad Finnegan didn't give us any trouble when we swapped out his supplies," Adina said, twitching like she couldn't stand the silence. "I don't think we need to worry about cleaning his clothes, though. He did come here to kidnap me, after all. And he was going to kill Kaia."

"And it would be unwise for us to allow him out to bathe," Penelope agreed. "And I certainly don't want to clean someone else's dirty underwear. Help me with this water, will you?"

Adina stepped forward and helped her pour the water into a barrel. Then the two of them lugged the heavy thing to the spring just outside the clearing.

"When do we worry about the others?" Adina asked.

"At dusk."

"I'm already worried."

Penelope watched the ripples on the spring as though some invisible creature was sneaking up on them. They quickly scooped up the water and backed away from the edge of the spring; the ripples disappeared.

"I'm sorry that you're worried. I am, too. But they needed to fill a lot of things here, so we can't start running around looking for them just yet." Penelope heaved the pot with both hands as Adina looked out at the swamp with a distracted expression on her face. "Come on. We need to get back."

Adina turned and hurried after her.

Kaia and Wickham were the first back, toting a large crate filled with herbs, roots, and other plants with them. The two looked utterly exhausted and covered in grime but beamed widely at Adina and Penelope. It appeared they weren't holding onto the tension from earlier in the day.

"We found potatoes!" Kaia exclaimed.

Penelope's mouth watered at the thought of roasted potatoes. "Excellent! Let's get a stew cooking for when the others get back, then."

It wasn't much longer before Lena, Jalene, and Herja returned. They each carried a crate filled with plants, nuts, and berries. Herja was in a low mood while Lena and Jalene explained how they had almost gotten a partridge, but a kelpie had snatched it from them and nearly grabbed Herja at the same time.

"Kelpies shouldn't be out during the day," Herja said when Penelope asked if she was all right.

They had just sat down to eat when an arrow whizzed through the air, striking the ground at Adina's feet. She yelped, throwing herself backward. Penelope jumped to her feet; her hands curled into fists as she looked around for where the arrow had come from. There was a slight disturbance at the top of an oak tree, but she saw no sign of anyone else.

"There's a note," Wickham said. "*Hand over the girl, and we will forgive the death of our captain.*"

"But he's not dead!" Kaia called.

Penelope shook her head. "They won't be able to hear you. I didn't think of them being in the trees! Shoulda built the wall higher."

Her mind raced. They were out in the open, with nowhere to run. Sure, they could open the wall, but how many of them were there? Was this an attempt to drive them out of their safety? Or would they shoot the students one by one until only Adina was left?

"We need weapons!" Adina grabbed up a thick branch and brandished it into the air. She twisted around and tossed it to Penelope. "We can use these—"

"No," Penelope said, distracted as she tried to think.

Lena made a noise of protest. "We can't just give up! After everything we've been through—"

"The moment we hold weapons, we become threats," Penelope warned. She threw the branch back into the woodpile. "They know we can't fight them back effectively, not unarmed as we are. But as soon as we arm ourselves, they will be justified in using more force against us."

"So, what do you suggest we do?" Adina demanded.

"Give me a moment." Penelope circled on the top, squinting as she peered around the camp. "Look to the trees; see if we can find them. And listen. You are the ones who will actually be able to hear if they're coming close."

Everyone fell silent as they obeyed. Penelope tried to ignore the whimpers of distress around her. As much as she would like to reassure the witches that everything would be fine, the truth was that this was precisely why she'd wanted to leave.

If they had left, they wouldn't have had much of a head start, but at least they wouldn't be sitting ducks like this!

We aren't sitting ducks. We're students of the Eldavon Institute. We're witches and dragons. Just because I don't see a way out of this, doesn't mean there isn't one.

"I don't see anything," Wickham said, breaking the tense silence. "They must be waiting for us to do something. But how will they know if we do anything if they're just waiting?"

"And why not just barge in here in the first place?" Adina added. "They've had no problems before confronting us. Why would they feel the need to send messages now? Are they really afraid of us? Do they really think we killed Finnegan? Maybe we should let him out and—"

"No," Penelope, Kaia, and Jalene all said at the same time.

Adina twisted her hands, her gaze now locked on Penelope's face. "Then you need to hand me over, don't you? Before anyone else gets hurt?"

"That seems backward. You'll get hurt, so it won't be nobody that gets hurt," Herja said.

She was the only one who hadn't been scanning the area for where the arrow had come from. Instead, she had remained crouched down. Only now did she straighten, and Penelope folded her arms in irritation. What was she on about now?

"I have an idea," Herja declared, then waited.

Penelope made a mental note to tell her that dramatics weren't appreciated, especially in the middle of a situation like this. "What idea?"

170

"We lure the Odentia into a trap, thereby stopping them from continually hunting us. But it's not without risks. Everyone will have to agree to work hard and fast if this will work."

Penelope nodded once, hoping Herja would continue with no further prompting. They couldn't keep waiting around, not when the Odentian warriors could be preparing to storm their little refuge.

"Adina, you'll have to be bait," Herja said, turning to her. "And you'll have the book bag with Finnegan in it. I know it's not ideal, but I want them to think that you're trying to escape and that you're taking him with you."

"But they think he's dead," Adina protested.

Herja shook her head. "I don't think so. If they really did, they would have no reason to continue bargaining with us. It would be most logical to assume that Row killed him. But if I'm right, the warriors would have been watching us since this morning. Which means they saw the work Pen and you did with the bag. I might be giving them too much credit, but I think we can count on them knowing we have Finnegan as a prisoner."

"And this is your plan?" Penelope asked. Her eyebrows scrunched up. "For Adina to run off with Finnegan alone?"

"Leading them away from the rest of us, yes," Herja said. "Then lead them back around to that deep mud where the foxtails grow. In their armor, they'll be too heavy and sink in. And the rest of us will have whipped up some cages or net bags or something, and we'll keep them prisoner until the adults get here. Simple."

Simple and impossible. Penelope couldn't see how that was going to work. But, right now, she didn't have any better ideas. They could remain sitting here until the Odentian warriors attacked, at which point there was little they could do to defend themselves.

It was a poor plan... but it was also their only plan.

"Alright. Adina, do you agree to this?"

Adina, pale and shaky, nodded.

"Then Herja will go with you. I don't want you out there on your own. We don't have supplies to make net ropes... we'll have to figure out how to make a giant cage." Penelope tried to visualize how they would do that and what time they'd need to accomplish it. "If this doesn't work, though, we go on the run."

Everyone nodded.

"Alright," Penelope murmured. "Let's get what we need, then. Adina, Herja, get ready. This is going to be hardest on the two of you."

ADINA FELL to her knees with a cry. Herja bent beside her, lifting the other girl back to her feet. Both were panting and shaking with how exhausted they were. Time didn't seem to have any meaning, but they needed to push on.

"Remind me never to listen to one of your plans again," Adina moaned, leaning heavily on Herja.

Between Adina's weight and the weight of the book bag, Herja wasn't sure how much further she could go. It had to have been at least four hours that they'd been running through the swamp. There didn't seem to be any sign of the Odentia now, though...

"Let's take a rest," Herja said. She helped Adina to a low log and swung her book bag off. Her clothes stuck to her skin with sweat, making her itch terribly.

"Thanks." Adina unscrewed her waterskin and drank from it. "Do you think we should loop back now?"

"Soon. I—"

An arrow whizzed between them. It sunk into a tree and quivered there. Adina shrieked, jumped to her feet, and started running again. Herja, who had been reaching for the message tied to the arrow, let out a strangled yelp and followed her.

"Wait," Herja shouted. "We forgot—"

She turned to go back for the book bag. But the Odentian warriors were already there, surrounding it. They tugged at the strings, and Herja knew she was right. Somehow, they'd figured it out.

Finnegan crawled from the bag, face red, spitting angry words. As he stumbled to his feet, Adina grabbed Herja's hand.

"Come on," she screamed. "We have to get out of here!"

Herja ran.

CHAPTER
TWENTY-SIX

The water beside the deep, muddy section of swamp rippled disturbingly. Wickham eyed it worriedly, not liking the look of it. He was sure he'd seen the shape of the kelpie that had tried to snatch him hovering below the water. When he'd pointed that out, though, nobody else saw anything.

A heavy thunk and a sharp cry made him jump. One of the thick logs they'd been trying to tie together with vines had broken free, swinging down to hit Kaia.

Wickham rushed over while the others hurried to secure the log.

"Are you all right?" Wickham asked as he knelt beside Kaia. She was tucked into a ball, her arms over her head.

Wickham pried her arms off when she didn't answer and looked at her scalp. Blood was everywhere, staining her hair red. He winced as he tilted her head up and checked her pupils. They reacted normally, which was a good sign. He quickly wadded a bandage over her scalp and looked up at Penelope.

"I need to get her back to camp and give her a healing spell."

Penelope nodded, looking concerned. "Be careful, though. We don't know when the Odentian warriors will be on their way back."

"Of course."

Wickham tried to lift Kaia, but his arms started trembling before he had even gotten her entirely off the swamp floor. So he adjusted his hold so he could help her walk instead. Mentally he kicked himself—this was why he needed to be stronger!

They were halfway to the camp when a horrible rattling sound reached his ears.

"Oh, no!" Wickham gasped, freezing.

Kaia had been resting her head against his shoulder as they walked, and she lifted it. "What's—"

She cut off when the bushes parted. The gigantic head of the Emerald Rattleback poked through, its tongue flicking out and in. Both children froze, and Wickham's mouth fell open. A shout, to frighten the snake away, was in his throat before he caught himself.

The Rattleback swung its head back and forth, then began slithering forward, ignoring the two. Its movement was sluggish, its brilliant green scales duller, somehow. Wickham drew Kaia closer, trying to put himself between her and the snake.

"It's all right," Kaia murmured. "We're not near its nest... it doesn't care that we're here. It's beautiful."

Wickham couldn't say that he agreed with that... he never did like snakes. But as it passed, a flash of brighter emerald green caught his eye. A gasp stifled in his throat. "Look! It's molting. If we can get some of that skin...."

Kaia, one hand on top of her head to hold the bandage in place, stepped forward. Wickham yanked her back as she reached toward the snake, but her fingers caught some of the loose skin all the same. It peeled back, easier and cleaner than peeling the husk off a corn of cob.

The body slimmed down into a feather-crested tail, showing it wasn't the same Rattleback that had attacked them earlier and disappeared. Kaia was left holding a large patch of shed skin. It was hard and leathery, unlike the delicate sheds Wickham had seen from smaller snakes. When he experimentally bent a portion at the top, it stayed fully intact.

"You think this will be enough for all of us?" Kaia asked as she held up the skin.

"Hopefully," Wickham replied. He took it from her and carefully folded it over his arm. "But we need to get back to the camp now. That bleeding hasn't stopped yet."

Wickham hurried Kaia along, hoping their incredible luck in catching this bit of shed skin wouldn't be for nothing... that the others would return victorious soon, and this trap would work. Because if it didn't?

It has to. And that's all there is to the matter.

"RUN, RUN, RUN, LITTLE GIRLS," Finnegan called after them, and Herja grabbed Adina.

"I can't," Adina sobbed.

Herja growled as she dragged the witch along; they'd barely had a single minute of rest before Finnegan's calls became audible again, showing he was far too close for comfort. "We're almost to the mud pit. We have to keep going!"

Adina flagged behind. "Leave me. I've only messed everything up anyway—"

"There's no room in this job for self-pity," Herja snapped at her as Finnegan's laughter rang in her ears. "Now move your butt!"

Adina made a strangled sort of noise but sped up, keeping pace with Herja now. They crashed through the swamp, not bothering to be careful; any disturbances they made now would only help them. But even the brownie nest they had disturbed some time ago didn't seem to slow Finnegan down by much.

They had to be almost there by now. Herja prayed she hadn't somehow gotten lost...

Then the bushes opened, and there it was—the slow, bubbling mud stank of sulfur and poop. The two girls nearly ran straight into it, and it was only because Adina pulled Herja to the side that they avoided getting stuck in their own trap.

Only now they had a problem that Herja hadn't thought through. "How are we going to get across?"

Adina took her hand and led her around to the side, pointing out a series of rocks and logs. "We'll have to be quick so Finnegan doesn't see."

She took a huge jump and landed on the first log as delicately as a butterfly, then skipped and hopped gracefully across. Herja was quick to follow, analyzing the surfaces before each jump. Soon, she was on the other side, next to the clear, beautiful pond.

Only nobody was in sight. There was no sign of a trap.

"We've come to the wrong place," she whispered, her heart dropping. And as the brush moved and rustled, she knew it was too late... Yes, this trap would slow Finnegan, but he'd be too smart to slog through another mud pit!

"It's hopeless," Adina said. She sank to her knees, her head bowed.

Herja couldn't find the strength to stop her.

The first few Odentian warriors emerged from the bushes. They charged into the mud pit, and the thick mud swallowed up their boots. They sank to their knees, and the force of their own momentum pitched them forward. The next warriors were too smart, though, and started edging around the pit, trying to get their comrades out.

When Finnegan emerged, his face was red; his lips pulled back into a snarl. He'd gotten himself another sword, which he pointed across the pit at the two girls.

"Leave them," he bellowed as he circled the pit. "I told you I heard their plan to lure us into a mud pit; if they're too stupid to listen, let them drown."

Several of the warriors gave him incredulous looks. One removed his boots and rolled up his pants, then strode into the mud pit to seize the fallen warriors. Finnegan stared at this warrior, his face turning purple with rage.

"What did I just tell you?" he howled. "I told you to leave—"

"And I heard," the man snapped back. "If you want to charge me with insubordination, go ahead. But I'm not letting anyone die on this fool's errand of yours, boy!"

"Oh?" Herja taunted. "Your own warriors can't stand you, huh?"

"Shut up, you silver-eyed brat." Finnegan leaped and landed on the first stepping stone. "I'll deal with you first, and then I'll deal with you," he turned and jabbed the sword toward the other warrior, "when we return triumphant, and my brother gives me all he promised."

A splashing noise started in the pool behind them. Herja turned slightly. A dark shape lurked beneath the water, then disappeared. It happened so quickly that she almost thought she had imagined it.

"Kelpie," Adina whispered.

How could she know? But the signs were there. Herja took a breath, said a silent prayer, and pulled Adina back to her feet. She needed Finnegan on this side of the pit, along with the rest of his warriors. They were making their way across now, being more careful than their leader.

"You don't have to 'deal' with anything over here," Herja said, dropping her shoulders and head to make herself look smaller. "I'm sorry about the crack I made about your warriors... I hoped that if I made you angry, it would turn you against them, and we could escape."

"Back up, into the tree," Adina whispered, her breath so light Herja could hardly hear her. They inched backward.

Herja took a deep breath. "You're too strong for us... if you promise not to harm us, or our friends, we will surrender."

Finnegan made the last jump to solid ground. He laughed. "No promises, brat. I don't need your surrender anymore."

Adina glanced upward and let out a small gasp. Herja couldn't help herself, looking up as well. Penelope, Lena, and Jalene were in the branches above them. Shock rippled through Herja. They were in the right spot, then... but why didn't Penelope and the others build traps for the Odentia? Where were Wickham and Kaia?

The waters in the spring churned harder, drawing the attention of the warriors at the back of the group.

"Don't think you can escape into the trees," Finnegan hissed. "I'm so sick of this place! Time to end it!"

He charged forward.

PENELOPE SWUNG DOWN, hanging over the branch by her knees as she dropped the rope. It fell right between Adina and Herja.

"Grab it!" she shouted.

"Grab it," Adina repeated, sounding frantic.

Both Herja and Adina grabbed the rope; Penelope released it at once, knowing she wouldn't be able to help from her position. Lena and Jalene grunted as they hauled the rope upward. Penelope could barely see Finnegan's expression change from disbelief to outrage. He opened his mouth, but it was silent to her ears.

The canopy seemed even more silent than the rest of the marsh.

From where she hung, Penelope could see Finnegan clearly. She took careful aim and threw the rock in her hand. It sailed past his head and landed with a splash in the pool next to him.

Herja braced herself on a lower branch and helped to boost Adina higher into the tree. Even as she did so, Adina gasped.

"They're going to burn the swamp down!"

"No, they're not," Herja said.

Penelope pulled herself back into a sitting position. From where she and Herja were, both could see the pond, and the kelpie, as it rose from the water. They stared at the magnificent beast.

It looked like a mighty war horse, coal-black with seaweed for a mane. Water glistened like diamonds as it dropped its back. It reared back, flashing fanged teeth like a wolf's.

Then it lunged. Penelope had to turn her face away.

"What's happening?" Adina demanded. She clapped her hands over her ears, looking terrified. "What is that?"

"It's a kelpie," Herja said.

Penelope nodded. "It attacked us and destroyed our trap just as we were finished setting it. Every time we try to get out of this tree, it comes back. When we saw you two coming, we thought maybe...."

She glanced down again. The Odentian warriors were trying to fight the kelpie, but their blades splashed through as though it was made of water—which it was.

In only a few moments, it was all over. The Odentians had all been dragged into the pond, and the water became still and calm once more. Penelope felt a rising sense of dread as though she had just done something unforgivable.

"So... they're dead, then," she murmured. She inched back toward the trunk, her heart leaden.

"No. Not dead."

Her head shot back up, and she stared at Herja. "What?"

"Kelpies don't kill their prey. At least not right away. They keep them underwater in sort of oxygen-rich mucus thing and come back to it every so often to feed... on their blood." Herja stared downward, her expression troubled. "But even if they were dead, we didn't kill them."

"We might as well have killed them since we led them into this trap," Penelope argued.

Herja closed her eyes.

"What were we supposed to do, though?" Adina asked.

"I... don't know." This crushing feeling squeezed her chest. She was supposed to be saving lives, not ending them! Not letting them end. "We can still get them out, though, can't we?"

Lena made a protesting noise. "And then Finnegan will kill us."

"Maybe his warriors will stop him."

"Or maybe they won't."

Penelope dropped from the tree, landing lightly. "I can't let them die."

Herja landed beside her.

"I need a plan," Penelope said, turning to her. "Tell me how I can save them."

CHAPTER
TWENTY-SEVEN

"I don't suppose I'll be able to change your mind?" Herja grumbled as she finished tying the rope around Penelope in the fashion of a harness.

Penelope eyed the clear waters, knowing the shallowness of the pool was just a deception. Her hands shook with knowing what she would face down there, but she was determined. She didn't want to be the sort of person who just abandoned other people to death, even if they were as bad as Finnegan.

"No," she replied.

Adina and Lena stood by, watching with concerned gazes. They worked on various vines the group had collected, turning them into a bundle of ropes to tie up the warriors. Jalene had gone to let Wickham and Kaia know what was happening.

"Be careful." Herja took Penelope's hand and squeezed it lightly. "You're my friend, and I care about you."

Penelope smiled at her, trying not to show her emotion. "I'll be back before you know it."

With that, she waded into the pool. It seemed to suck her down like the water was heavy mud. Taking a deep breath, she dove into it. Instantly, the world seemed dirty and black. It stung her eyes, so she squinted them, pulling herself along the roots and bramble stuck in the pool's bottom. The water got colder as she got deeper.

A shadow passed by her.

Penelope froze, her eyes shooting wide open. But everything was so dark; she couldn't see a thing. Something slimy brushed against her foot; she kicked and met only hard roots. Her lungs screamed for air, and her head spun, even though she knew she shouldn't be out of breath yet.

Something tugged on the back of her shirt, and on impulse, she went limp. It would be impossible to find the kelpie's store here on her own. But if she let it take her there…

They were suddenly moving so fast it made her stomach lurch. The rope snapped tight around her, and for a second; she was afraid it would break. Then, something warm surrounded her. She tried to push it away, but it wrapped around her, sucking her in like mud.

Mud… she was in the mud pit!

The air in her lungs exploded. Penelope tried to stop herself from breathing in, but her body wouldn't listen. To her shock, her lungs easily drew in air. Though she felt liquid all around her, none filtered into her mouth.

Penelope relaxed her body, not fighting against this heavy feeling anymore. She had to conserve her strength. What had Herja told her again? A thick, mucus-like substance. Kelpies surrounded their victims with it. It allowed them to breathe underwater but also kept them immobile.

Now came the hardest part of the plan… breaking free from a substance meant to stop the captives from breaking free.

Penelope slowly pushed her arms outward. If she moved slowly enough, the resistance was lessened to a point where she could move, but it wouldn't be enough. She focused on her gut and recalled all the descriptions her family had given her of the first time they breathed fire.

Usually, it was only after they had shifted for the first time… but there was no time to wait.

She pictured a ball of fire in her belly and imagined it blazing like the inferno of a forest fire. It whipped to a frenzy, looking for the only path out. She dropped her jaw and heaved, shooting flames through the thick mucus surrounding her.

It melted off.

Immediately, the water rushed to take its place. Penelope clamped her jaws shut as she clawed her away free from the mucus, her lungs burning once more.

Quickly! No time to lose! But in this darkness, how could she find the Odentians? The rope tugged around her middle. Panic seized her. She couldn't go back yet! She hadn't found them! But she was being dragged backward...

Her hand brushed a clump of mucus. And Penelope did the only thing she could do. She reached out and wrapped both arms and legs around the form inside. The rope tightened, her grip slipping on the mucus bulb. Then something seemed to break free, and she moved smoothly, holding the mucus in her arms.

But her lungs were screaming for air, and everything was so dark...

"FASTER!" Herja yelled, pulling the rope. Her eyes remained fixed on the kelpie pool, her heart pounding in her ears.

Mistake, mistake, mistake, Herja's mind seemed to say. *You've killed the only person in this entire world who can put up with you.*

Penelope's head broke the surface of the water. She inhaled, then let out explosive coughing. It was all Herja could do to keep pulling on the rope inside of wading in to help her—she knew that would be a mistake; it would make her vulnerable...

But she wanted to get in there, to pull Penelope out of the water.

"Heave!" Herja shouted, giving a mighty pull. "Harder!"

Penelope kept coughing. Her tanned skin tones were turning red. Slowly, trying to pull her from the mud, Herja and Lena put their weight into it, dragging Penelope out of the water.

It soon became clear why this was so difficult as a large bulbous, sticky mound the color of fresh vomit emerged along with her. Penelope's limbs were tangled in the mound, which twitched and bubbled as though something was trying to get out from inside. More and more mucus bulbs kept coming out of the water.

A horse's head peeked from the pool. Its ears were pinned back, its wild eyes focused on Herja. Everything seemed to freeze as their gazes locked. Water dripped from is midnight black fur. Her hands remained tight on the rope, slippery and wet with the swamp water.

The kelpie shrieked as it lunged froward. Its fanged flashed, water splashed all around. It charged Herja, its stone hooves digging in the mud—

Flames burst into the air, eating the distance between Herja and the kelpie. She screamed, stumbling as she dropped the rope. A terrible caterwaul rang in Herja's ears. The Kelpie reared back, kicking out toward her.

Herja threw herself back.

Something strong caught her. As she whirled around, a fresh scream arose, and her eyes latched onto a familiar sight. Row. All the air left Herja's lungs, and she collapsed against the Professor, uncontrollable sobs shaking her whole body.

AS IT TURNED OUT, Penelope rescued not only all the Odentian warriors but also an entire herd of tiny swamp deer from the kelpie. Herja almost felt sorry for it. The kelpie wasn't evil, per se. It was just a being whose existence differed from theirs.

They had come into its home, after all. Disturbed its life.

Herja lay on her bedding after the first full meal she'd eaten in what felt like forever. The dozen or so adults had taken over the camp, insisting that all the students rest. They would have gotten to the students sooner; only the Emerald Rattlebacks had been in rare form, hunting down all dragons to repeatedly bite them, preventing them from taking dragon form.

"We'll fly you all out in the morning as soon as dawn breaks," Row said from where they crouched near the fire.

The Odentian warriors currently lived in Herja's bookbag again. One witch that accompanied the search party had cast a spell to increase its internal size to hold all their prisoners.

"What about Lee and Icarus?" Wickham asked anxiously.

"What about the scouts that were sent before?" Penelope followed up.

"What about my parents?" Adina asked.

Kaia waved her hands at them even as Row and the other adults smiled at the children. "Be quiet and let them answer."

"Lee and Icarus were taken to the Mount Eldavon hospital," Row said, first facing Wickham. "They're going to survive. Icarus will have a long recovery ahead of him, but Lee has already returned to the Institute. He still has to rest, but he's well enough to get back to life."

Wickham's smile dropped to his chin, and he closed his eyes like he was praying. Gratitude, Herja supposed.

She rolled to her back and closed her own eyes. "He recovered that fast once he was in the hospital?"

"Once the bleeding in his brain was healed, yes."

Herja bolted upright, her eyes snapping back open. "Brain bleed?"

Row nodded, expression calm. "If it weren't for Wickham's herb mixtures and healing spells, he would have died in a matter of hours. We all owe you, Wick. You saved Lee's life. And as for Icarus, I'm sure the same will be found."

"Oh, my goodness," Herja whispered. She pressed both her hands to her cheeks. She'd known it was bad, but... it seemed she had underestimated Wickham's abilities. She glanced over at him, a newfound respect welling in her heart.

"Now. As to the scouts we'd sent when we first learned King Diesel had passed," Row continued.

At this, Herja glanced at Kaia. She had known King Diesel personally, after all. And during all this mess, neither Herja nor Penelope had taken the time to check in with her to see how she was coping with his loss.

Kaia wrapped her arms around her knees and laid her cheek against her arm.

"Finnegan attacked them all, just as he said, with Rattleback venom on his weapons, preventing them from shifting to their dragon form. However, he didn't kill them. They escaped into the swamp and distracted the warriors as long as they could until they were forced to retreat once more. All of them are dealing with injuries, but there were no deaths."

Herja let out a sigh of relief. No deaths. It was more than she had hoped for. Even the Odentian warriors taken by the swamp had been recovered. Although... that was one more question she had.

"What's going to happen to Finnegan and his warriors?" she asked.

Row paused in their tending of the fire. Their eyes dropped to the glowing coals, and something twitched in their expression. But what did it mean? "Finnegan is one of the younger brothers of the Odentian king. He claims that he never sent Finnegan, though, and has told our kings and queens to execute him in payment for these crimes."

Herja shuddered.

"His own brother?" Wickham asked in shock.

"Is he going to be executed?" Lena asked, trembling.

Was that why there was that twitch in Row's expression? Were they really going to execute him?

"No," Row said, and Herja sighed in relief.

Even though she didn't want to believe Eldavon would execute anyone, she realized how much about the world she didn't know... and she had a feeling that there was a lot about Eldavon she didn't know, either.

It was good to have faith in this part of the Kingdom, though... in justice.

"He'll be imprisoned?" she guessed.

"He will, yes. At some point, we may release him back to Odentia. It's difficult to tell, however. But that is a matter for—"

"Our political leader?" Herja interrupted. "That's what you were going to say, right, Row? You would not say that it's a matter for adults since apparently kidnapping and all that is a matter for children... not that we're really children anymore. Teens, yes. Children—"

"Children, yes," Row interrupted. They leaned over to swat Herja's nose playfully. "You'll understand once you're older. When you reach certain ages, everyone under another age remains babies and children. I call my nineteen-year-old brother a child still."

Herja stuck her tongue out at them. "If we're children, you're an olden."

"Olden?" Row repeated.

"Yup. Olden."

It occurred to her suddenly that she didn't really make up words like this. It all felt like a childish exchange, the sort that would always make her roll her eyes at others at the orphanage. And yet here, now, it felt right.

"You should all try to sleep," Row said, smiling at the group. "Don't worry. You're safe."

Safe. It was a pleasant word. Herja relaxed into her bedding again, letting her eyes drift shut. Safe. It was a delightful word indeed.

CHAPTER
TWENTY-EIGHT

Though all the students at the Institute were invited to Queen Abigail and King Sydney's Coronation, Adina extended a personal invitation to the other first-year witches, along with Herja and Penelope.

Though Kaia loved beautiful dresses she could wear to parties—they were too impractical for day-to-day life. Though she would have worn a ballgown to class if she could—she couldn't muster up much excitement for the event. It was a glad time for the Kingdom, knowing that their future was safe in the hands of the new king and queen...

But it also felt like the Kingdom had grieved for Diesel and moved on before she knew he was gone. It felt far too early to have a new coronation, let alone a celebration.

Queen Charlize must be so sad. Kaia wished she could talk with the old queen but she hadn't attended the Coronation. Maybe she could sneak away from the party unnoticed at some point.

"Doesn't Abigail just look so beautiful?" a nearby human sighed. "She has such a commanding air about her."

Kaia moved away from the excited chatter. Though the palace courtyard was beautifully decorated, she found herself being quiet and withdrawn while her classmates spread out. Several government workers had come to ask her about the incident in the swamp, and she'd avoided talking about it for so long.

Maybe she really should sneak off to see Charlize.

Kaia was lingering near the fountain, pretending to be entranced by the splashing waters, when Adina approached her.

"Hey," Adina said. She wore a dark blue tunic and trouser combo with a black jerkin over it. "You look distracted... is everything all right?"

The last thing Kaia wanted was to bring Adina's joy on this occasion down so she forced a smile. "Lost in thought is all. And how about you? I haven't seen you in class this last week."

Adina smirked. "I was allowed to take a break to help mentally prepare for all this." She waved her hand around. "I wanted to thank you, Kaia. You didn't have to be as kind and understanding as you were in the swamp. I know I got pretty whiny."

"I wouldn't call you whiny," Kaia protested.

"I would."

Kaia laughed as she shook her head. "Alright, fair enough... but we all got whiny. It makes sense, given the circumstances we found ourselves in."

Adina nodded to where the other first-year witches were. "How about we go join the others? I wanted to see how Icarus was doing, anyway."

Kaia followed her to where the others stood in a loose circle. Wickham offered her his napkin with a handful of sweet treats on it. Kaia picked one out and tasted it.

"So what are we talking about?" she asked brightly.

Icarus gave her a shy smile. "Well, me, I guess. I'm not being expelled from the Institute. I also won't be joining in next year's quest, at least not until I've had a review done. But I'll be permitted to rejoin classes after the winter break."

"That's good news," Adina beamed. "And your health?"

"Fit as a fiddle. At least I feel fine. The doctors still want me to take it easy," Icarus amended.

Wickham lifted his glass of orange juice. "And you should listen to them. You were cut open with a poisoned blade. You don't know what sort of lasting damage—"

"Wick," Kaia complained.

He blushed and fell silent.

"Um..." Kaia felt the lull in conversation weigh on her. Even though she wasn't super invested in this party, she also disliked the silence now... it felt too much like dwelling on everything that was wrong. "Icarus, I heard your parents were returning to Odentia?"

Icarus picked at the food on his plate. "Maybe. They're in discussions about whether they will take a position as ambassadors to Odentia since they are citizens. They haven't decided just yet. The situation is complicated, you know."

"Sorry," Kaia said miserably. "I didn't mean to upset you."

"They'd be perfect for ambassadors, though," Penelope offered.

Herja nodded. "At least they know what Odentia is like culturally and are less likely to make a faux pax that will anger the old king."

"But there's also the possibility that they could be called spies and traitors," Icarus replied. "And, of course, they were never from the high classes; it's not like they know the ins and outs of court and all that. All the same, I hope that things will change... the old king has accepted some supplies for the spring plant, at least."

Kaia's thoughts turned to Finnegan. She had heard nothing about him in the last few weeks... but he was most likely still locked up. Would his brother call him a traitor for returning without the prize he'd been sent for?

"Don't know why we're offering them help," Lena grumbled.

"Because the people are starving, and they're not responsible for their idiot king," Penelope replied dryly.

At least the armies had retreated... Kaia rubbed her eyes, not liking this new world-weary feeling that had come over her. She had a feeling that she would have a harder time trusting the world now; her image of life had been changed, and nothing could change it back.

Wiser doesn't mean I have to be gloomy all the time, though. I just need time to adjust. Kaia let out a small sigh. Yes. Time to adjust, mourn, and figure out life again. She would not let this keep her down, but she needed time.

One of the first-year dragons, Nolen, approached the group. He looked uncomfortable but handsome in his dark suit. He bowed stiffly toward Adina, then turned to Kaia.

"I heard you enjoy dancing," he said.

Kaia nodded. "Most times, yeah."

Nolen's dark silver eyes skirted around the room. "I don't know how to dance. Could you teach me?"

Kaia hesitated. She still wanted to sneak off and pay her respects to Charlize. On the other hand, this was a celebration. She could find Charlize tomorrow, and then they could have a better conversation. If Kaia knew the old queen, she would insist that Kaia go back to the party and enjoy herself.

"I can teach you," she agreed finally, holding her hand out. "Though I'm sure there are others who would be much better at it than me."

As she led him onto the dance floor, her mind suddenly flashed to fated mates again. At the end of the next school year, they'd find out who their mates were. She was a witch, and Nolen was a dragon. Was it possible?

She pushed those thoughts aside as a strange, fuzzy warmth filled her chest. There would be time to think about all that later. Right now, she just wanted to have fun with a friend.

Because that was all Nolen was—a friend.

PENELOPE SLIPPED into the powder room, finding a nice, low couch to collapse onto. Her feet ached with the hours of dancing she'd done already. Her hair must be a mess!

Near a vanity, a mirror was on one side of the room. Penelope headed over, tucked her hair back into place, and then stepped back to look at herself. When she, Momma, and Julie shopped for dresses, Penelope picked this one because it was simple and not too flashy.

Now, though, she thought of how absolutely stunning Kaia looked with her ruffles and ribbons and the flush in her cheeks as she spun in circles with Nolen.

Penelope turned away from her simple reflection. She leaned against the wall, fighting the wave of jealousy that washed over her.

She would never be as pretty as Kaia. Penelope never thought that she really cared about her looks that much. And yet, she couldn't take her eyes off Kaia tonight, with an unexpected yearning in her heart. Maybe next time, she would get a dress with ruffles and frills, too.

Everything seemed to change, and change... was frightening.

"Penny for your thoughts," a voice said behind her.

Penelope turned and frowned when she saw Herja. "Ha ha, hilarious."

Herja shrugged, looking utterly serious. "I just heard your parents talking about what happened in the swamp and how you've already got skills for the Fire Watch. It reminded me of a question I haven't asked because I respect your privacy."

Penelope arched a brow at her. "Why does that sound like you've decided to no longer respect my privacy?"

"Why are you joining the military rather than the Fire Watch?"

With a wince, Penelope turned away. There was nowhere to run, though, not unless she wanted to run back to the party.

"I'm going to keep asking until I get an answer; maybe not tonight, but there's always tomorrow and the next day and the next...." Herja let the threat hang in the air.

"It's not really any of your business, though," Penelope mumbled.

Herja shrugged. "I know I'm not helpful the same way Kaia and Wickham are. But I think these things are easier when you talk about them."

"I... I... I decided I need to. I can't really explain it, Herja. I just. Need to." Penelope pressed her fingers to her temples. "I can do more good in the military."

"And... you haven't told your parents because... why?"

"I don't want to disappoint them."

"But why would they be disappointed?"

Penelope lifted her head again.

Herja truly looked puzzled. She scrunched her nose as she thought. "Do your parents have something against the military?"

"Well... no, not really. I mean, I know they wish it weren't necessary, but given Odentia's behavior of late, it is necessary to have some sort of protective fighting force. But I've always said I was going to join the Fire Watch. My parents and both my siblings are part of the Fire Watch." Penelope spread her hands in a helpless gesture. "Now it's all going to change."

"I... don't see," Herja said. She came to sit on the couch, her nose still scrunched.

Penelope flopped onto the couch next to her. "I don't know how to explain it better. It's all so confusing."

"I can tell. But it's more than that, Pen. I never had people who have been really, truly disappointed in me. Or rather, I've never cared whether they were. Maybe it's because I'm an orphan," Herja shrugged. "I just think we have to figure ourselves out, you know? And pretending to be someone we're not just because it changes other people's perceptions... well, that's not good."

"Maybe I'm just too afraid right now," Penelope murmured.

Herja turned to her. "You're the bravest person I know, Penelope. Whenever you decide to tell your parents, I know it'll be just fine."

Penelope hugged her friend. It'll be just fine. She knew it would be... so what was holding her back? Change? Was that it?

Or is there something else that I just can't verbalize right now?

CHAPTER

TWENTY-NINE

Wickham rubbed the cramp in his hand, wincing as the muscle pulled and tightened. He hadn't realized he'd been grinding the herbs so much until he had taken a break from doing it.

It was the first week of winter's break, and he was picking up his first shirt at Kassandra's shop. Kassandra sat at her mixing table, carefully measuring ground herbs into separate concoctions. She moved with such deftness, not even glancing at her spell book. It amazed him.

"So, you figured out healing spells enough on your own to keep two critically injured patients alive, huh?" Kassandra asked abruptly.

"Uhhhh..." Wickham flushed as he stared at the herbalist. How had she found out about any of this? He'd told his parents what had happened, but they had promised not to tell anyone else.

Kassandra handed him a pamphlet. "The society pages. There's a huge expose about the Silent Marshes and everything that happened there. Most of the information is focused on Adina and Kaia, but you've got quite a mention, too." She smirked proudly.

Wickham skimmed the pamphlet, flushing harder. "No. Why would they print this? Why wouldn't they tell me to talk to them? Who printed it anyway?"

Kassandra laughed. "Reporters, writers, I don't know. People want to know what happened, so you have official and unofficial means of finding out about it. Anything you want to tell me about your adventures?"

Wickham let out a heavy sigh. "I don't think it was much of an adventure. Terrifying, exhausting, and... it wasn't fun. Adventures should be fun."

"You want to talk about it?"

"Not really. I ended up asking the, uh, wounded individuals for permission to look at their medical reports—cranial swelling in one, Rattleback venom in the other. I didn't know what I was doing. I just thought of how you heal injuries and tried to mimic it the best I could." Wickham frowned as he picked up the mortar and pestle again. "I need to learn better diagnostics. The Institute won't teach me that sort of thinking."

Kassandra hummed. "There's always medical school."

Wickham nodded. "Only after I graduate, though. And if next semester is anything like this last one, I will need more immediately. Besides, if I get some training, I can work at the Institute's medical wing and earn more money."

Kassandra hummed again.

"You always make that noise when thinking of something deep and important," Wickham said.

"Ah. Thank you, I didn't know that. No wonder I never win at poker."

Wickham rolled his eyes.

Kassandra chuckled. She finished measuring out the last ingredient and then drew the drawstring of each bag, sealing it tight. "I just thought you have a genuine talent for healing, Wick. And I am certain you will quickly outstrip what I can teach you. It will serve you well to train with the medical staff at the Institute."

"And?" Wickham pressed, sensing there was more.

"And... how are you about leaving your family, now? As I recall, you had a few things to say about it at the beginning of the semester."

Wickham flinched. Oh, yes. He remembered his emotional

outbursts well. Funny how having his life threatened in the swamp should have made it even more difficult to leave his family again. He should be more determined than ever to stay home to look after them...

"Once we were attacked in the swamp, I couldn't keep thinking about them all the time," he finally admitted. "I had to focus on helping other people. And I think it changed something."

He fell silent for a moment, sorting out his own thoughts. It wasn't easy for him to admit any of this, really. For so long, his primary goal—his only goal—was to take care of his parents and siblings, even though they didn't need him to care for them.

"I've learned that some people really need to be taken care of," he said slowly. "And I still want to help my family. I want to make sure they're healthy and taken care of. But I think they don't need me. At least, not right now. Not the way I want to be needed."

"Is that so?" Kassandra asked.

"Yeah. That's so. At least, I think that's so," Wickham told her. He had to stop grinding herbs again as his hand was acting up. "Besides, the more I learn and the better connections I develop, the better I'll be able to care for them when they need me."

Kassandra laughed aloud. "That's a good point there, Wick. Now. I've given it some thought and will start teaching you more advanced herbal magics. Nothing huge, mind you, but enough that you can figure out your own spells for that book of yours."

Wickham straightened. "Really?"

"Of course," Kassandra stood. She stretched her back and picked up her cane. "Of course, it will be intensive learning. You will have to put in longer hours here, and I expect strict, diligent work."

"I would give you nothing less," Wickham replied. He stood as well, his eyes shining. "Can we start now?"

"Not right now, no," Kassandra said as she handed him the bags she'd just finished measuring out. "Run along and deliver these to my grey-haired patients. It's an arthritic medicine to help with those aches and pains. I'll have the first lesson prepared when you return."

Wickham took the bags and carefully stowed them into the pouch at his hip. "Thank you, Kassandra."

Kassandra waved her hand at him. "Yes, yes. Now get going."

But she smiled, and her cheeks turned pink. Wickham turned on his heels and headed out, already making a mental list of questions to ask his mentor. He had much to learn—and was eager to learn it all.

KAIA STRETCHED out on the rug before the fireplace; her chin propped onto a pillow with a book in her hands. The schloss was always too drafty for her liking, but there was something delicious about resting near the fire.

But only when I have four walls around me. I never want to go camping again.

An icy breeze hit the side facing away from the fire, heralding the door's opening even before she heard the sounds of entry. Kaia dropped her book and rolled herself into her blankets, hiding away from the cold.

"Shut the door," she cried out.

"Sorry, pumpkin," Mama called back.

The door shut, and soon footsteps sounded in the family room. Kaia pulled back her blanket wrapping to find her parents entering the room. She sat, her eyes widening as she took in the both of them.

"I thought you were busy," she blurted.

Mama and Papa sat on each side of her, holding their hands to the fire. Kaia could feel the cold still clinging to them and shuddered. Oh, she was starting to truly, deeply dislike the cold. Why did it have to be so... *cold*?

A glance passed between her parents. It was a strange glance, with minor changes around their mouths and eyes, as though they were having a private conversation right before her. They had these sorts of conversations quite often... but Kaia never liked them.

"Tell me," she begged. "Don't just do that quiet talk thing."

"Well, dearest, we talked over what you told us," Mama said slowly.

Kaia frowned. "What did I tell you?"

"About how you felt abandoned in the swamp and wished we were there," Papa said gently.

"Oh," she mumbled. She ducked her head. "I know it was silly."

"Dearest, your feelings are never silly." Mama hugged her and kissed the top of her head. "We were so worried about you. But we never thought you would feel that way. And while there wasn't anything we could do at the time, I believe the incident might be pointing to a larger problem."

Kaia shook her head quickly. "No. It's not."

Papa gave her a knowing look. "Your mother and I have worked a lot these past few years. You've been such a happy child that I don't think we really noticed how often we were gone. That's going to change. Your mother is taking an extended vacation so the three of us can have your full winter's break together."

"Mama... but what about your work?" Kaia asked, shocked.

Mama waved her hand. "Pshaw. My work will be there when I go back. There isn't much to be done in winter, anyway. Besides, you are more important."

Kaia snuggled against her. At fourteen, she knew she was getting a little too old for this cuddling, but she didn't care. She didn't feel all that grown-up, after all. If she did, maybe she would like these changes that kept happening to her body.

She didn't want to be 'all curves' like her mother. She wanted to be like herself. She wanted to fit into her favorite dresses still instead of having to get all new ones because the seams in the bust popped out.

She shook those thoughts aside. Papa had said Mama would take time off for her winter break. "Does that mean you'll be working over the break?"

Papa shook his head.

"Then... what?" Kaia asked.

"I've decided to retire and take on a consulting role," he replied. "I'll work while you're in school; otherwise, I'm staying home with you."

Tears burned Kaia's eyes. She didn't even know this was what she needed until now. But even though she was happy and could imagine all the fun things they would do together, some small part felt guilty.

"I don't want you to give up your career for me," she mumbled, slightly turning away so they wouldn't see her watery eyes. "And what about the Kingdom? Don't they need you, too?"

"We have to balance what we give to the Kingdom and what we give to our families," Papa said.

That same strange look passed between him and Mama again. The sort of look made Kaia think they were keeping secrets from her. But what sort of secret could it be? Maybe they were afraid that Finnegan would somehow still come after her.

Actually, that made perfect sense to her. He had been released from the Eldavon prison and sent back to Odentia on the king's insistence. He would probably be furious when he got there... and he was just the sort of person she could see trying to get revenge.

The thought made her shiver again, but she exaggerated it as though she was cold. Finnegan couldn't hurt her here. She was home. Her parents were here. Her tutors lived in the schloss, and she had a bigger extended family than anyone else she knew.

She was safe here. Nobody was going to hurt her again. She didn't have to fear Finnegan.

But it would be a long time before he stopped haunting her dreams.

CHAPTER

THIRTY

"There's nothing like a good hot meal after a day playing in the snow, eh Pen?" Benton asked as he shook the snow from his hair.

Penelope nodded happily, taking off her knitted cap. She had just spent a wonderful day with her family in the Fire Watch camp. Work didn't end with the snow, but it certainly helped to calm down the major fires that the Watch was still battling. The smell of roast made her stomach rumble as she hurried to wash her hands.

Momma and Da were already at the table by the time she and Benton sat down, and last of all was Julie. She'd been doing this often, showing up late to family activities. Her witch-mate was spending more time with them, too, though, and Penelope liked the energy he brought to the family.

"Since we're all here on this beautiful winter's day," Da said as he sliced the roast. "Does anyone have any exciting things to share?"

"I do," Julie said with a grin.

Benton served himself potatoes. "Nothing for me."

Nerves hit Penelope's stomach hard. She had been trying not to think about the change she had made to her future, but here she was, with the perfect opportunity to tell them.

"I have something important to share," she blurted before she could lose her nerve. "It's not exciting... in fact, I had a hard time coming to this decision, and I... I didn't want to share it for a while, but I must say it before it gets more difficult."

Julie's smile faded. "Can it wait?"

Penelope shook her head. "It can't. You see... I will not join the Fire Watch when I graduate."

Momma and Da shared a startled glance. Julie and Benton both frowned at her.

"What are you talking about?" Julie demanded. "Of course you're joining the Fire Watch. That's all you've talked about since you were tiny."

Penelope fought not to hide inside herself. No, she didn't want to have this conversation, but it still needed to be said. "I know. But things have changed. I need to be somewhere where I serve the Kingdom differently. I knew from the moment that the Odentian spies first kidnapped us. I'm joining the military."

"The military?" Julie leaned back in her chair. "What do you think you can do in the military?"

"I can serve the Kingdom by defending our borders and giving aid in the places where I need to be," Penelope replied.

Julie made an angry noise. "You can do that in the Watch. What are you even thinking? This isn't you, Penelope. You don't want to go around killing people! Or do you? Do you want to fry them to a crisp while—"

"That's enough," Da thundered.

Julie fell silent.

"Julie, I will not have you disparage our forces. It is unfortunate to have an army, but so long as there are other kingdoms that would take our resources by force, it's a necessity." Da took a deep breath and resumed carving the roast. "You're still young, though, Penelope. You have lots of time to decide about your future."

"I know. But I've made my choice already."

Momma opened her mouth, then closed it again. She slowly stood. "Penelope, I understand that this is something you've thought of, and thank you for sharing this. I would hate for you to think you can't talk to us. I am going to need a few minutes to collect myself. But I love you."

"I love you, too," Penelope said.

She watched her mother as she left. She slumped back in her chair. Well, this could have gone better. She'd known it would surprise them that she had planned to joined the military, but she expected none of this.

Disappointment sucker-punched her so hard it hurt. Tears blurred her vision, and she kept her head down as she served herself food.

"You always said I could do whatever I felt was best," Penelope finally said when she couldn't stand the silence anymore.

Julie made another furious noise. "That doesn't mean you get carte blanche to make a stupid, selfish—"

"Julie!" Da shot to his feet. "Outside. We have to talk."

When Da got that tone, you didn't argue with him. He marched outside, and Julie shot Penelope a venomous glare before she also stalked away.

Penelope clenched her fists in her lap, struggling not to cry. What happened here? Why was Julie acting so angry? Why did Momma have to leave like that? She opened her mouth to ask but didn't want Benton to abandon her, too. So she remained quiet.

"Hey. You know it's just because they're worried, right?" Benton said.

Penelope scrubbed her eyes.

"First the kidnapping on Mount Eldavon and now the attack on the Silent Marshes. They're just worried that there's going to be a full-out war coming. And if you're part of the military, it means you'll be right at the forefront of it."

"I already am." Penelope finally lifted her head and met her brother's concerned gaze. "I was kidnapped. I was attacked. I faced down trained warriors with *nothing*. You can't imagine how terrifying all of that was. But my only thought was to protect my classmates. Because this is what I was made for, Benton. To protect."

Benton sighed. "I didn't mean to infer that you don't understand the dangers, Pen. I just... was trying to explain why Momma and Julie would react that way. Honestly, I want to do a little shouting myself. But it's only because... because you were kidnapped. You were attacked."

Fresh tears spilled down her cheeks.

"You faced down trained warriors with nothing. You stood between swords and your classmates. You encroached on a kelpie's lair to save the very people who had attacked you." Tears rolled down Benton's cheeks now, too. "You're a beautiful soul, Pen. And war is ugly. We just don't want to lose you."

"I'm sorry," Penelope hugged him, sobbing.

Benton patted her back. "I know. Just as I know you've got to make your own choices, I'll support you every step of the way, Pen. I promise."

It wasn't the four expressions of support she had hoped for...

But one was better than none.

THE NET HUNG BELOW HER, promising a soft landing if her fingers slipped off the bars like they had done so many times before. Herja grit her teeth as she undulated her body, building enough momentum to swing to get the next bar. Her muscles screamed at her, but she powered through.

"That's it," Row called encouragingly from somewhere below her.

Even though she really ought to be calling them 'Professor Farrow' again, Row hadn't told her to stop calling them Row, and so she didn't. It felt nicer, somehow.

Herja reached the last bar. Now she would have to swing herself forward and release the bar at just the right time to fly across the gap and land. Her breathing was harsh to her own ears, but she swung back and forth, building her momentum higher.

"You can do this, Herja," Row reassured her.

She released the bar and flew through the air. Her feet touched the platform—and her body tilted backward. She windmilled her arms, trying to catch her balance, but it was too late. She tumbled back, hitting the net. She bounced, then lay still, catching her breath.

"Well done," Row said as they came to the edge of the net. "You almost made it this time."

"Almost doesn't count," Herja grumbled.

She pulled herself off the net, frowning up at the swinging bars.

Row laughed. "Almost counts. Every effort you make counts. Now let's go back inside. Twila will have my head if she knows I let you run the course in this cold weather."

Herja snorted. "But it's not even icy."

They headed inside the Institute. Herja wasn't the only first-year student staying over for the winter break, but the place certainly was quiet. She hadn't thought she would miss the noise and activity, but she did.

Or maybe it was her friends she missed. Penelope, Kaia, and Wickham.

Her friends.

Friends who liked her, even though she could be annoying.

"I forgot to ask, could you salvage your book bag?" Row asked once inside, making their way to the dining hall.

"The swamp mud stained it pretty badly, but at least it doesn't stink anymore. I tell you, it smelled so bad. Who knew a bunch of warriors covered in kelpie excretions would smell like that?" Herja wrinkled her nose, nauseated at the memory. She made a beeline for the fireplace and sat beside it, holding her hands to the warmth.

Row headed into the kitchen and returned a few minutes later with two mugs of hot cocoa. They handed one to Herja and sat down in the overstuffed chair. "That bag of yours certainly has come in handy. I'll bring it up to Lantos and see if he thinks they can be recreated for the army."

"I'll never get used to you calling him just by his name," Herja muttered. She sipped her cocoa, then held the warm mug to her cheek. "Do you think I have what it takes to be a queen one day?"

"Unequivocally," Row replied without missing a beat.

Herja frowned. "Do you think I have what it takes to be a good queen, then? Do you think it's a career path I should pursue? Or am I just kidding myself?"

Row gazed into the fire with that thoughtful, calm gaze they had so often. "I believe you could make a very good queen, Herja. You have skills that would be good for the crown and good for Eldavon. But you need to consider what sort of queen you want to be. Agricultural? Military? Medical?"

Herja considered their words, leaning back. It wasn't something she had considered before, but the kings and queens had a distinct part of the government they oversaw.

"Working with Penelope made me realize that I'm not a natural leader," she said eventually. "How can I be a good queen if I'm not a good leader?"

"You learn."

"How?"

Row hummed. "Spending more time with Penelope would be a good start. Observing what she does. But also realizing where your strengths lay and what you need to do with them."

"What if my strengths are better suited to making Penelope a queen?"

"Does she want to be a queen?"

Herja shrugged.

"Then no. Your strengths aren't better suited to making someone queen who may or may not want the job." Row stretched their arms over their head, still looking into the fire. "I will tell you this, though. Even Lantos falls back and lets others take the lead when he knows they're in a better position."

"Meaning...?" Herja pressed.

Row's lips twitched. "Meaning, you know Penelope has been part of the Fire Watch all her life. She knows forests. She also did a great job keeping everyone together and unified last year at the Silver Springs. So, you stepped back and did what you needed to do to ensure she could use her strengths to their full advantage."

"I don't think so."

"I do."

"But if I had done it, wouldn't I know I'd done it?" Herja challenged.

Row only smiled at her. "Do we always know why we do something as we do it?"

Herja groaned. "I wish you'd just be clear in what you're saying rather than always having to be a mystic riddle dragon professor hermit."

Row chuckled.

"I need to learn how to use a sword."

Row's humor died away. "That's not my area, and you're—"

"A threat as soon as I have a weapon in my hand, I know," Herja replied. She met Row's eyes and set her cocoa aside to fold her arms. "But here's the thing. Finnegan would have hurt or killed me regardless of whether I'm a threat. So, I want to know how to defend my friends if this happens again—and you can't say it won't. It's already happened twice."

Row rubbed their face. It appeared they were hovering on the brink of saying no, but then they nodded. "Very well. I'll start teaching you. But you do not touch those weapons without supervision. Understood?"

Herja sipped her cocoa again and grinned. "Understood, Professor."

Next time, she'd be prepared.

Next time, she would protect her friends.

Next time, she would not be afraid.

The End

If you enjoyed this book, please consider leaving a review on Amazon, Goodreads, or Bookbub.

Reviews help me reach new readers.

Read **The Quest for the Sacred Tree**, the second book in the **Defenders of the Realm** series!

OR

Read **A Summer of Discovery**, the first Fantasy Romance Novella in the **Defenders of the Realm** series!

Have you read the prequel?
A Journey to Power

Join my Newsletter for writing updates, sales and giveaways!
www.mhlebeault.com

www.ingramcontent.com/pod-product-compliance
Lightning Source LLC
Chambersburg PA
CBHW032002240626
47153CB00003B/1084